TUCK
TRIUMPHANT

TUCK
TRIUMPHANT

THEODORE TAYLOR

DOUBLEDAY
NEW YORK   LONDON   TORONTO   SYDNEY   AUCKLAND

All of the characters in this book are fictitious,
and any resemblance to actual persons, living or dead,
is purely coincidental.

DESIGNED BY PETER R. KRUZAN

PUBLISHED BY DOUBLEDAY
a division of Bantam Doubleday Dell Publishing Group, Inc.
666 Fifth Avenue, New York, New York 10103

DOUBLEDAY
and the portrayal of an anchor with a dolphin
are trademarks of Doubleday, a division of
Bantam Doubleday Dell Publishing Group, Inc.

Library of Congress Cataloging-in-Publication Data
Taylor, Theodore, 1922–
Tuck triumphant / Theodore Taylor. — 1st ed.
p.   cm.
Summary: Fourteen-year-old Helen, her blind dog Friar Tuck, and
her family face some dramatic challenges when they discover that the
Korean boy they have adopted is deaf. Sequel to "The Trouble with Tuck."
[1. Dogs—Fiction. 2. Adoption—Fiction. 3. Deaf—Fiction.
4. Physically handicapped—Fiction.] I. Title.
PZ7.T2186Tu   1991
[Fic]—dc20   90-3195   CIP   AC
ISBN 0-385-41480-3

ALL RIGHTS RESERVED
PRINTED IN THE UNITED STATES OF AMERICA
MARCH 1991
FIRST EDITION

I want to express my gratitude to Mitzi Carver, counselor for the California School for the Deaf, Riverside; to Sally Larrimer, teacher of the deaf; and to Twila Scott, Sulphur Ranger Station, Granby, Colorado, for their help with research.

Theodore Taylor
Laguna Beach, California

FOR SHEILA QUINLAN,
Trainer of Guide Dogs

TUCK
TRIUMPHANT

1

There was still one dangerous, reckless leftover, something that frightened all of us, from the days when Friar Tuck Golden Boy was a sighted, free-running dog, apt to roam all around the neighborhood and his favorite haunt, Montclair Park.

The leftover was an occasional jaunt without his guide dog, Lady Daisy, or me, Helen Ogden.

Having been hit by a car almost in front of our house not too long after the light faded, you'd think he would have learned a lesson. Not so. Behind those gooshie gray eyes was always an independent and defiant "I'll show you" spirit.

I have in mind a Tuesday afternoon in March when I returned from school to find Lady Daisy alone in the backyard.

Calling for him, I looked around inside the house,

thinking he'd used the dog door to go back in. I looked in every room. No Tuck.

Daisy had followed me and I said, "Where is he?"

Her tail wagged but that wasn't much help. That tail wagged a lot for one reason or another. I did a second search of the house and then returned to the backyard. He'd been known to gather speed and take a flying leap over the back fence, clearing it from memory, I guess. Dogs do have memory capability, probably better than any other animal.

It was about three-thirty, an hour and a half before dark, and I went back into the house, wrote a note to Mother saying Tuck was loose, leashed Daisy and took his leash along. Off we went in search of that stubborn Labrador.

This was the third time since we'd acquired Lady Daisy that Tuck had gone off on his own, and twice before we'd found him in the park, doing what he could spend hours doing—sniffing every tree trunk and bush. Just how he navigated, safely or not, crossing Denham and going on into the park, was unknown.

Of course, there are many known cases of dogs travel- eling miles, even hundreds of miles, back to their homes. Cats too. But I think those animals were sighted and used the combination of sight and smell to return to their families. Tuck had only the latter, of course.

True, he knew his way along Cheltenham, having marked it with urine day after day, but getting across Denham was another matter and I could only guess that he "heard" his way across, waiting until all car noises were gone, then hurrying to the next curb. I could almost see him doing that.

But it was a dangerous thing to do and I'd reacted with a mixture of fright and anger the other two times he'd run away. I just wanted to get my hands on him.

It took less than a minute to cover the three quarters of a block, cross the street and get into the park. I went by the fountain with Daisy and looked everywhere, even standing up on the edge of the pool, getting some added height, shouting his name. No sign of the yellow dog.

Then we started off in more or less his usual pattern of exploring, moving along Denham and going toward the Wickenham boundary, then turning back toward the Cheltenham boundary.

Whoever I passed, I asked, "Have you seen a big yellow Labrador?"

I got "no" answers.

"He's blind," I said.

"Sorry," was what they said.

Yes it *was* a sorry state and the sun was sinking lower over Los Angeles with every minute. Soon the rush-hour traffic would be building up on Denham and every other street around the park. Cars often traveled Wickenham at forty and fifty miles per hour.

In the darkness the drivers would be lucky to see Tuck. He'd be lucky if they did see him. That miserable dumb hound! No, he wasn't dumb—just miserable.

"Where is he?" I yelled at Lady Daisy, angry at her for not stopping him, realizing at the same time that there was no way she could prevent him from jumping the fence.

I very seldom swore when I was in my early teens but I did that late afternoon. I damned Tuck every which way. It would be back on the chain for him and I knew how he hated those steel links.

Within ten minutes I knew he wasn't in the park and went straight over to Ledbetter's to ask greengrocer Mr. Ishihara if he'd seen the dog. Tuck well knew the route to the market. Mr. Ishihara shook his head.

Where? Oh, where?

Had he followed another hound away? A bitch in heat? Possible. He was very much a ladies' man and had yet to be spayed.

Had he been kidnapped? Pure-bred yellow Labs were targets for thieves but I didn't think he'd go along willingly with anyone.

Had he been hit by a car already and taken to a vet? Worse, had he been killed?

I began running along Denham, all of those thoughts whirling around in my head. I was beginning to get panicky. Anger was going away, a sick fright replacing it. After ten or twelve blocks on Denham I started back for the park to take another look there.

A steady stream of headlights went in both directions on Denham and cold darkness now transformed the park into an unfriendly place of deep shadows. With Lady Daisy at my side, I wasn't afraid of the shadows.

Again shouting for Tuck, I circled the park on a run

and then decided to go home on the chance that he'd returned.

Bursting into the kitchen, I said, "Is he here?"

Mother shook her head, saying, "I'm glad you're back. Do you realize how dark it is out there?"

"I'm going to find him," I said, trembling, tears beginning to fall. Though confident about most other things, I still got weepy over Tuck.

"Calm down, Helen," she said. "Your father will be home in a little while and we'll all look for him."

"He could be killed," I said, raising my voice.

"And he could also be perfectly all right," she said.

"We won't eat dinner," I said. A demand!

"No, we'll look for Tuck just as soon as he comes home."

"Where are Luke and Stan?" I asked.

"Upstairs, doing homework."

"They can help." Another demand! I was frantic.

"Yes, they can help. Why don't you sit down? You're perspiring."

I went over to the sink for a glass of water. "He's been gone since three, I know. I got home at three-fifteen."

"You've looked in the park?"

"Twice."

Then I heard my father's red MG in the driveway and went out, catching him as he was opening the car door.

"Tuck's gone," I blurted.

"Again? Oh, jeez," he said. "I don't need that tonight."

"He's been gone more than three hours."

Daddy said, tiredly, "Helen, sometimes that dog is such a pain in the royal tail. Let me get my coat and tie off."

I followed him into the house. He kissed my mother and before she could say anything, he said, "I know, I know. Another search party. Someone leave the gate open or did he jump the fence?"

"He jumped the fence," I said.

"I want him on the chain for a while," he said, exasperated.

Tears came down again as I said, "If we can ever find him."

Luke went with my father in the MG and I rode with my mother in the station wagon. They took the section south of the park and we took the area north of it, driving around block after block until almost seven-thirty. We spotted a few dogs but not Tuck.

Finally, my mother said, "We have to give up and just hope he comes home. We could ride around all night and not find him."

"Where could he have gone?" I said, racking my brain.

Mother said, "You just have to trust he'll come when he's ready."

"But he can't *see* to come home," I wailed.

"We all know that," she reminded.

When we reached 911 West Cheltenham the MG was parked in the garage. My father and Luke had given up.

In the house, Daddy said, "We tried, Helen, and I've called Dr. Tobin at home. Let him know that Tuck is missing." Dr. Tobin was our vet.

One of the collar tags was stamped with our name and phone number on one side, Dr. Tobin's on the other.

"He said to tell you to have faith. He thinks Tuck'll find his way. I do too."

After dinner I put on a heavy jacket and went out to sit on the back steps. Daisy came out with me and curled up by my feet. Stars were out by now and three quarters of a moon was in the eastern sky. Sometimes I got up and walked down to the end of the driveway, looking off toward Denham and the park, listening to the night noises.

He was out there somewhere, maybe confused, uncertain how to find our street, our house. Lost!

I must have prayed a dozen times that night.

Finally, about ten o'clock, my mother opened the kitchen door and said, "Time to go to bed, Helen. There's nothing you can do out here."

"I can wait," I said. I was half-frozen.

"You can also wait in bed."

Getting up, Lady Daisy tagging behind, I climbed the stairs reluctantly, went to the bathroom and off to bed, knowing I wouldn't sleep. But I dozed now and then, I think.

About one o'clock in the morning a bark that I knew so well speared into one of the dozes and I jumped out of bed, took the steps two at a time and ran through the kitchen, opening the back door.

There he was, outside the gate in the pale moonlight, wagging his tail furiously, big grin on his face. He was fine.

Opening the gate, I said, "You bad dog," but knelt down to hug him. His fur was cold, as was his nose.

Suddenly, I realized that others were looking on. My mother, my father, Stan. Then Luke joined them. Daddy shook his head tiredly and said, "Now, we can all get some sleep."

Many dogs had done the same thing, gone off on a jaunt, but this time was an exception: this dog couldn't see the end of his nose.

Where had he been for more than ten hours? With a female? That was Tuck's secret and none of us would ever know.

Would he go off alone again?

2

There were those who said that blind dogs were totally useless and should be put to sleep, the kind that lasts forever. They were wrong and I can prove it many times over.

There were those who looked down at Tuck's dead-fish eyes, patting him on the head, saying, "Poor dog, tch-tch-tch-tch," pitying him. Pity was the last thing that tough wandering canine ever needed.

I'm sprawled out on my antique white-iron bed in my childhood room on West Cheltenham Avenue, looking at two photographs and thinking back a long time as I tell my second story of Friar Tuck Golden Boy.

One photo shows a girl of thirteen—me, Helen Ogden—kneeling between big Tuck and Lady Daisy. The latter was then six and a half years old. Tuck was five. He'd come into my life as a squirming ball of fur.

In the other photo, along with the dogs and a

fourteen-year-old "myself," is Chok-Do Choi, a little Korean boy, grinning crookedly straight into my father's camera. He has his hand on Tuck's head. Oh, how he loved those dogs.

Looking closely at both of those blown-up, grainy prints, I see a freckled, red-haired girl with a puggy nose, mouth too large for the jaw and enough wire bracing in her teeth to set off an airport security alarm. She's skinny, has spindly legs and knock-knees. Her glasses have lenses as thick as Coke bottle bottoms and sometimes mean kids called her "Goggle-Eyes."

As I recall, very painfully, Goggle-Eyes was definitely not the prettiest thing in Montclair.

Why couldn't I have looked like my mother? I hated the scrapbook pictures of her when she was twelve and thirteen, especially several with good-looking boys. Why couldn't I have looked more like my best friend, Steffie Pyle? Being flat-chested at the age of fourteen is a total disaster.

To make matters worse, my brothers were true "jocks." That's the only way to describe them. Football and baseball and basketball players and blond surfers rippling with muscles. No wonder they had plenty of sexy girlfriends.

Whenever I was unfortunate enough to stand between them, a matchstick-in-the-mud between two jewels, I wanted to dig a hole and drop through to the Himalayas.

Just vanish. *Poof!*

Anyway, that's how I looked on my five thousand two hundred and eighth day on earth.

As might be expected, neither dog showed the slightest excitement when I told them, that early June, about the Korean boy we were adopting. Friar Tuck just sat there, dripping pink tongue hanging out, massive yellow head pointed toward the sound of my voice, as usual.

"His name is Chok-Do," I repeated. "He'll be here in three weeks. What do you think?"

The sightless eyes just stared at me.

Lady Daisy simply yawned; then her tongue rolled out.

It was my youngest brother Luke who said of me, "She's crazy, all the time talking to the dogs." The older, nicer brother, Stan, didn't call me crazy.

Well, millions of perfectly sane people talk to their dogs. Millions of perfectly sane people talk to their cats. Hundreds of thousands talk to their horses. Others talk to hamsters and gerbils and so forth. The animals may not exactly understand but they sense something. If nothing else, what they sense is love.

So I often talked to Tuck and Daisy about matters of less importance than Chok-Do Choi. Boyfriends, teachers, my parents, Luke and Stan, Elvis Presley, boyfriends, boyfriends, of which I had none.

Why not talk to my dogs—share my innermost secrets? They were usually around me, padding along every time and everywhere I went, except off to school. They slept by my bed and sometimes *on* my bed, making a warm canine sandwich with me in the middle.

My love affair with Tuck had begun the first day I met him, two days after he was weaned, when he was eight weeks old. Sometimes I thought I loved him more than I did my parents. In a way, I loved him more than I did my brothers, who weren't contributing much to my life at this point, especially Luke.

My love affair with Daisy, a German shepherd, had begun the day I first saw her at the California Companion Dogs for the Blind School. All she needed to do was look at me with those soft doe eyes.

So it was natural and easy to talk to them.

That sunny day was no exception, I remember. I took them over to Ledbetter's Independent Market, on Rosemont, five blocks away, on a milk and bread run and also to tell my good friend Mr. Ishihara that we'd just heard that Chok-Do would soon be arriving.

Mr. Ishihara had been my adviser on the training of Tuck. He was the one who suggested cutting off my unlaundered shirttail and using it as a lure. Tuck sniffed it, picked it up in his mouth, and I then began the long process of persuading him to put his head up against Daisy's right rump and guide on her, eventually without a leash.

That was *the* key element in training my thick-skulled Lab to let Daisy be his "eyes." Success came after months of heartbreak.

But those two dogs were now a familiar sight around our neighborhood, going everywhere together, crossing streets, Daisy waiting patiently for traffic lights to change. Then off they went, bell ringing on Daisy's collar so Tuck could hear her as well as smell her. That was another Mr. Ishihara suggestion.

After guiding for humans, Lady Daisy proved that she could do it just as well for her own kind, and those remarkable two were now minor celebrities, having been on TV and in the newspapers. In fact, it seemed to me that sometimes I was lost in all the hoopla about them. You'd think they'd trained themselves. Fat chance.

Mr. Ishihara was in front of the store out on the sidewalk by his vegetable stands, which were always inclines of beauty. Reds and greens of peppers, glistening stalks of celery, shining tomatoes, misted-over each day. In season, every imaginable vegetable was displayed there. He took as much pride in his greengroceries as my father did in his electronic circuits; my mother in successful students.

My father was an engineer; my mother taught fourth grade. He was pudgy, bespectacled, balding and fatherly, no candidate for *Playboy* ads. She was auburn-haired, green-eyed and had a good figure for her age.

I said, "We heard about Chok-Do Choi. He'll be here in three weeks. He has to go from his little village to Seoul to catch the plane."

The smallish man with the short, crisp gray hair and radiant smile, always wearing a black bow tie and white apron, said, "That's good news, Helen. You should start practicing to speak Korean."

He slipped Tuck and Daisy a dog biscuit each, as usual. He kept them in a box behind the stands. Customer canines were always well-treated by Mr. Ishihara.

"Tonight I'll start," I said, knowing I wouldn't.

We'd bought an English-Korean phrase book. Their words are full of hyphens, *o*'s and *y*'s, very confusing to non-Koreans.

"Do you speak it?"

He shook his head. "Not even my Japanese is good. You remember, I told you I was born in Santa Monica. Japanese and Korean are two very different languages. We may look something alike but we're two different people."

Well, he'd be of no help in translating. Why didn't my parents adopt a boy from Canada or England? Better still, a girl. I already had two brothers. Why not a girl from the U.S.A.? I'd said that before and gotten hammered.

"My mother's been practicing Korean dishes for a month. To make him feel at home."

"Korean food is very good," said Mr. Ishihara.

It was okay. But what crazy names. *Kam-ja kook*, which was potato soup; *moo-sook-jang-ah-gee*, which was turnips with beef. Then there was *keem-chee*: pickled vegetables, which Mom said was served with practically every meal over there. *Keem-chee* burnt my mouth. No thanks.

I went on into Ledbetter's to buy the half-gallon of milk and loaf of sourdough and when I came out, Mr. Ishihara asked, "How old did you say he was?"

"Six." Barely.

"He'll learn English before you know it. A year, I'd bet."

"They're very smart, aren't they?" I said.

"They just work harder. Chinese, Koreans." With a twinkle in his dark eyes, he added, "Japanese."

I knew that. We had some Asians in school. They had the best grades. So now we were going to produce another Oriental genius. Right in our own house. I didn't need the competition, especially from a six-year-old.

A lady stepped up to buy two artichokes. It was late afternoon and dinner shopping for fresh vegetables had begun.

I said, "Talk to you later. I have to go."

Mr. Ishihara grinned. "Good luck with your Korean lessons. You can teach me. I don't use my brain cells enough."

I nodded and said, "Up, you dogs," and away we went, Daisy heeling on me and Tuck plodding behind her, Dudley-pink nose against her right rump.

We crossed Denham on a red light, heading home. Motorists smiled and waved.

I took a roundabout route back to West Cheltenham, stopping at Steffie Pyle's house to tell her about Chok-Do. We were the same age, went to the same school, thought the same about most things. The big difference between us was that Steff was pretty, with raven hair and good teeth, and her bust was growing. Also, there were live boys, not fantasy boys, in her life.

"My new adopted brother is arriving in three weeks," I said. "We finally heard today."

"The Korean?"

I nodded.

She put a gleam into her gigantic eyes and swished her lashes. "I wish he was older."

"I have enough problems with Luke. As I said before I was hoping for a baby. A six-year-old we don't need."

"You may learn to like him."

"He'll go his way and I'll go mine."

"Did they even try for a baby?"

My parents, of course. "They said they did."

Steff's mother, Alice, came in from an afternoon of playing bridge. I told her about Chok-Do.

"That's wonderful," she said.

"I guess."

I said I had to go on home and told Steff I'd call her in the morning. School was out for the summer.

Earlier, I said I didn't have any boyfriends when I was thirteen and fourteen. Unlike Steffie Pyle. To be completely truthful, I didn't have a boyfriend until I was almost sixteen, and he was a reject, like me, but the opposite. I was a stringbean and he was an Idaho potato. Plump.

Frankly, I was Miss Stringbean Metal-Mouth Goggle-Eyes and, quite frankly, he was a Lard-Butt. He jiggled.

Like rejects often do, I turned to fantasy. Friar Tuck would now be John Tuck, a junior at Montclair High. Almost six feet tall, a sunshine blond, he had a perfect body and shiny, straight teeth, the nicest smile.

One rainy afternoon in 1956, I put on the latest Elvis

hit, "Love Me Tender," and was dancing around my room with John Tuck, his hind legs on the floor and his front paws on my shoulders.

Luke came by, saw us and went to the head of the stairs to yell down, "Mom, come up and see what she's doing." He was laughing.

I slammed the door and locked it. I needed a strong and handsome lover and Tuck qualified.

Other times I might daydream, which is exactly the same as fantasizing, that Tuck was an Alps dog, digging down to rescue a skier after a Matterhorn snowslide. Or he could be locating trapped earthquake victims in San Jose; on the track of a lost child in the Sierras after having sniffed a sock. Sweat from human feet was the easiest scent there was.

Tuck could have located Luke's feet in a sold-out Dodgers stadium.

3

The *Los Angeles Times* had called Tuck's guiding on Daisy a "triumph" and KABC-TV had said it was a "joy to watch, darkness rolled back." I suppose it was all of that for them but now, a year after it happened, their moving about the streets and park had settled into dull routine, which was natural.

I still got letters from people with blind dogs, wanting to know how I'd gone about it. Answering each one, I told them all about Daisy and Tuck.

His family could be traced back to sixteenth-century England when Devon fishermen first invaded the shores of Newfoundland. On those boats were dogs, and they became known as Labradors. The third Earl of Malmesbury was the first to own a Lab of the original breed. So Tuck had ancient and aristocratic blood in him. He was every bit the "Earl" of West Cheltenham.

He still looked much the same as he did when he went blind, at age three and a half: powerfully built, with a wide chest and well-sprung ribs, loins that were heavy and solid. His hindquarters were muscular and his legs straight from shoulder to ground, with heavy bones. Paws compact, thickly padded, his toes were perfectly arched and hocks well-bent. The dense, short coat appeared to have been dipped in twenty-four karat gold. On his black bulb was that streak of pink that made him a "Dudley nose," not qualified for the show ring. Who cared? The only thing wrong with Tuck were those useless eyes.

But he was my special hero well before he lost his sight, saving me from a rapist out in Montclair Park, launching himself at that man like a wild bull; then rescuing me from the bottom of Steffie's pool. I'd struck my head on the diving board. Tuck had never been trained to do that sort of thing and Dr. Tobin said it was instinct, plus love, that sent him diving to the bottom, bringing me to the surface unconscious.

Lady Daisy? A little chubby, absolutely female, with the calmness and wisdom of centuries in her eyes, she led Tuck around as if he were a living caboose. Her breed of sheepdogs was even older than Tuck's line of hunting dogs. She'd been a guide dog for humans, retiring after her blind master died.

From puppyhood on, wearing a proud green and white vest that said "Companion Dog in Training," she'd learned how to cross streets safely, go on elevators and escalators, board buses and trains, move down busy sidewalks on a short leash, always alert and ready for action in face of danger. Tuck was so lucky to have her.

The only great physical change in Tuck—that I could see, from his pre-blind days—was in his hearing and sense of smell. Dr. Tobin had expected that to happen: sharper hearing, sharper sniffing to compensate for lack of eyesight. Apparently, Tuck could smell a passing dog a half-block away, hear leaves fall in the backyard.

Had the "triumph" of training Tuck and Daisy changed me?

Yes! A big shouted *yes.* I was no longer the poor petunia of eleven and twelve, weeping at any defeat, the miserable wilting daffodil, the shrinking violet of 911 West Cheltenham. I did not take to being pushed around anymore by Luke, who was almost sixteen, and Stan, who was seventeen. Now, I fought for my family rights. Nor was I a pushover at school anymore. I had confidence in myself, at last, and the psychologist gave all credit to the training accomplishment with Tuck and Daisy.

Though I still wasn't any beauty in face and body, I was confident, *which counted more,* I had to tell myself, fact or not.

I still whistled constantly but it was for pleasure now, not to combat fear. I liked to whistle the William Tell Overture and that marching song from the movie *Bridge over the River Kwai:* "Whee-how, whow, who, whee-whee, who . . ."

Tuck and all other modern dogs are the sons and daughters of the original wolves, even little dachshunds and Chihuahuas, amazingly. So he had a drop of wolf blood in him. My mother didn't exactly appreciate some of his burying places in her flower beds but knew it was the wolf's instinct. She said, "Oh, well," and shrugged.

And Dr. Tobin had been absolutely right when he said Tuck's nose would become more sensitive as a result of blindness. I had no idea that wolves and dogs have two hundred and twenty million smell-sensitive cells in their noses, while we humans have only five million.

Tuck's hearing sharpened, thank goodness, as Dr. Tobin had also forecast. He'd always been able to distinguish our cars from others just by engine sound, not at all unusual for a smart dog, know when one of us was coming up the driveway just by the sound of our steps. Dr. Tobin said that was because his hearing cycles were up to quadruple of humans, maybe eighty thousand or more, compared with our twenty thousand or so. Wolves can hear a howl four miles away.

4

Two weeks and three days had passed.

Mother said, "Helen, we're going to make some room changes because of Chok-Do."

She said, "Helen."

Oh, Lord. She didn't say Luke or Stan. *Helen.*

As I'd told Steff, a year ago I'd been all for adopting a "baby" when my parents casually said they'd been discussing such a thing. My mother said she thought she was too old, at forty-one, to bear another child. And why not help the overseas orphan situation? We all said that was a great idea. I did, in particular.

Being the youngest Ogden I'd never been around a baby.

"Great," I said at the time. Foolish girl.

Then, every so often, we'd heard about the progress. An application had to be filed, of course. Mrs. Gaines, from the church-sponsored overseas adoption agency, came by to inspect the house and meet all of us. Our lawyer became involved drawing up papers, as did the immigration office. Then, finally, one afternoon late in the tenth month, my mother beat me home to say, huge smile on her face, "This is your new brother." She was holding a photograph.

"His name is Chok-Do Choi." She spelled it.

My mouth dropped. "He's no baby."

"He's five years and ten months. Isn't he beautiful?"

He had a round face, black hair and big eyes but I wouldn't have called him "beautiful" at the time. I'd seen Mexican and Italian and Swedish and Thai boys who were lots prettier. Plain American boys too.

Disappointed, I said, "I thought we were going to get a baby."

"Obviously, we didn't," Mother said. "Your father and I have known for two months we weren't going to get a baby. But we're lucky to have Chok-Do."

What an awful name, I thought. Chock Full O' Nuts. Choco-late. Chock-O-Block. And "dough," as in lump, for a second name. Choi sounded like a tropical fish. Later, he'd be "Chok Ogden." Charles, maybe. Change his name.

Needless to say, I was demolished. All along I thought we were trying for a six-month-old or younger. Something I could hold in my arms. Something that felt and acted and *smelled* like a baby. I had my female instincts.

What we were getting was a half-grown kid.

I picked up my fork, waiting for the bad news.

"We've decided to move Luke in with Stan . . ."

Stan said, "Hey, wait a minute."

Luke protested. "I'm sleeping with *him*?"

"And, Helen, you'll take Luke's room."

"*Luke's room!*" I said. Luke's room? He had B.O. most of the time. He threw his dirty socks under the bed.

"So that Chok-Do can be right across the hall from us," my father explained. "He'll feel more secure."

Stan said, "Why can't he move in with Luke?"

"Yes, why can't he move in with Luke," I agreed, relishing the idea.

"With me?" Luke yelled. "Not with me!"

"Stop it," my father shouted. "I'm ashamed of all of you. There's a new child coming into this family and all I hear is selfishness."

Daddy seldom raised his voice to us and that made it more shocking. "Now, stop it," he demanded. "Do you hear?"

Stan looked at me and I looked back. Luke went from Stan's face to mine. All right, we were being selfish but our rooms were *our* rooms. Special places to be alone.

Mother said, quietly, "He's too old to sleep in with us. You should know that."

Sighing, I said, "What do I do, just leave my room the way it is?" My clothes, my furniture.

"Take whatever you want out of there. Your clothes, your books. It's not as if you're going away."

I shook my head in frustration.

Anger still on his face, my father said, "There are only four bedrooms. Something has to give."

Stan thought a minute and saw some hope. "My bed is a double."

Mother nodded. "I'm well aware of that, Stanley. I've made it up enough times. I ordered two three-quarters from the May Company last week. You'll both sleep well."

Luke asked, "How long will this last?"

Mother studied him. "I'd say until Stan goes off to college."

That would be more than another year.

"Oh, no," Luke groaned.

I decided to keep my mouth shut. There are advantages to being female. There were sure to be some fights up in what would now be called "Stan and Luke's room." Some real drag-out doozies.

"When does all this happen?" Stan asked, downcast in face and voice.

"You can stay where you are until the afternoon before Chok-Do arrives."

Two more days.

"Will Tuck and Daisy be with me?" I asked. A dumb question.

My father shook his head and sighed deeply, looking at me over his glasses. "Helen, I'm not into that decision. That's up to them."

"Up to the dogs?" I asked, glancing over at them.

Mother reminded, "You are not moving more than fifteen feet."

It seemed more than that. It seemed a mile.

"What about the bathrooms?" I asked.

"Chok-Do will use the boys' bath. You keep on using ours."

That was a break, at least.

Feeling low, I said, "Are we still going on the camping trip?"

Each summer we'd gone off to different places for two weeks, more or less. We'd done Yosemite, Yellowstone, Sequoia and Kings Canyon. This year we'd planned to camp Never Summer Wilderness, near the Rocky Mountain National Park, in Colorado.

Daddy always had a month's vacation from his engineering company, spending about two weeks in the mountains, then taking a romantic week away with my mother—no kids going along—and then a final week working around the house and yard.

"Yes, of course," he said. "I think Chok-Do might enjoy Never Summer."

He'd better, I thought. Colorado was going to be something special. At least, for me.

Luke came by my room later on that evening to say, "I almost wish that kid wasn't coming here."

I didn't say anything but felt the same way.

"Maybe Immigration won't let him in."

"Maybe," I said.

"Or maybe he won't like it here and ask to be adopted by someone else?"

I said, "Maybe."

He nodded and went next door to his room, which would soon be mine. There are a lot of tennies on earth that stink but Luke's were the worst.

Taking Tuck and Daisy downstairs and out to the backyard for a johnny session before bedtime, I said to them, "You can sleep wherever you want." I didn't mean it.

I was still angry about being kicked out after thirteen years in that room.

5

"Will that adoption lady be here?" I asked again, wishing I were somewhere else. At very best, I'd gone along with this whole thing halfheartedly, hiding my true feelings, since learning we weren't getting a baby.

Here was the old, tottering Los Angeles airport of my childhood, mostly wood and corrugated iron. A new one was being built.

Mother shook her head. "She called yesterday. She had to go to Salt Lake City. We're on our own, Helen."

We'd survive, I thought. As usual.

There was a family poem that we all recited on appropriate occasions. Birthdays and such.

> *We are the Ogdens*
> *Tougher than leather*
> *We are the Ogdens*
> *We stick together*

Stan had written it when he was about ten and now thought it was silly. He was embarrassed by it.

After a while passengers from Pan Am Flight 12, a three-tailed, four-motored Constellation, began to come out of Customs and Immigration, relatives running to meet them, hugging and kissing, jabbering, laughing. Most of the passengers were carrying packages wrapped in straw. The greeters had bouquets of flowers.

I'd left Tuck and Daisy at home, telling them this was the day their new brother was arriving.

The rest of us Ogdens—father, mother, Luke and myself—stood silently watching for *our* passenger. Finally, we saw a pretty Korean stewardess holding the hand of a little boy who looked even younger than six. On his chest was a big sign: Chok-Do Choi. In his right hand was a small straw bag. In her free hand the stewardess held a little gray stuffed koala.

Chok-Do was a war orphan and war orphans usually had few possessions. The fighting between North Korea and South Korea hadn't been over too long.

He's beautiful, I thought, flat admitted it. I melted at the sight of him, unlike the new me.

He was wearing a white shirt and his dark shorts were held up by suspenders. Beneath sturdy legs, shiny black shoes were on his small feet. His black-black hair was crew-cut and his face was as round as a lemon pie and about the same color. Truly beautiful.

I glanced at my mother and saw tears. I saw that my father was dabbing at his eyes. Luke was swallowing.

Why were we all so sad? Then I suddenly realized my own eyes were wet. I couldn't believe myself.

We moved to meet him.

Smiling widely, the stewardess said, "You are Chok-Do's new family?"

My father said, "Yes, I'm Tony Ogden."

Mother was already kneeling down, hugging her new son, kissing him, saying, *"An-nyŏng-ha-shim-ni-kka."*

"How are you?"

We'd all learned a little Korean.

Then she stood up, wiping her eyes, introducing the family. "This is your father and this is Helen, your sister, and this is Luke, your brother."

Bewildered, he looked at us as if we were Martians, saying nothing. His eyes were huge and brown and I was wishing they were mine.

"Do you have identification?" asked the stewardess.

My father quickly displayed the adoption papers and his driver's license.

She glanced at them and then seemed to be sizing up Chok-Do's new family, going to each of our faces, an inquisitive look on hers.

Finally handing over his Korean passport and a visa, she said, in almost flawless English, "Well, I have delivered him as I promised. I must say I admire your courage to adopt a little deaf boy."

She glanced down at Chok-Do and smiled.

I heard my mother gasp and then my father said, in a squeezed voice, "What? What did you say?"

"Deaf boy?" Mother said. "There's some mistake." On her face was shock, disbelief.

"Weren't you told?" asked the stewardess. "He does not hear, does not speak."

Staring at her and then at Chok-Do, my parents answered together a breathless: "No!"

"I'm sorry," said the stewardess. "I wish you good luck."

Then she knelt down by the boy, kissed his cheek, smiled briefly, handed him the koala and disappeared back into Customs and Immigration.

Daddy called after her, "Wait a minute!"

Mother said she had to sit down and went over to a low concrete-block wall, taking Chok-Do by the hand. My father went over and sat down beside her. They were in a state of shock. So were Luke and myself. So much for the tough Ogdens.

Riding home, Chok-Do sitting in the back between Luke and me, looking out the window at his new homeland with wide eyes, little hands on his knees, my mother said, "What do we do?" She barely whispered it as if the boy could hear and understand: speaking to no one, speaking to all of us.

Daddy said, in a normal voice, "Barbara, I don't know. We'll call Mrs. Gaines in the morning, find out whether or not she was aware of the problem. I doubt it very much . . ."

He stopped talking and took a breath. "I honestly don't know what to do."

"Do we . . . !" My mother then took a deep breath and started again. "Do we send him back?"

He sighed. "Barbara, I honestly don't know. Maybe we can't."

Then my mother sighed. "I hate institutions but I don't know how to cope with this if it's true. The Korean part, him speaking no English, was something I thought we could handle but I don't have the slightest idea about deaf-mutes . . . I don't . . ."

Her voice trailed off.

Daddy said, absently, "They're trying not to call them deaf-mutes anymore. Hearing impaired, I think."

Luke and I stayed silent. The thoughts and questions we had, and there were many, were better left for another time. We could feel the anguish of our parents.

Nonetheless, I put my hand on Chok-Do's and he looked up at me, unsmiling. I realized how frightened he was: taken out of an orphanage, put aboard a noisy airplane for a long overseas flight, then handed over to four strangers. Even if he wasn't deaf, all of that would be frightening to any six-year-old. Terrifying, if you thought about it.

After a drive that continued mostly silent, we arrived at 911 West Cheltenham, going up the driveway on the left side of the house, stopping by the kitchen entrance, as usual, none of us having given a single thought about *who* and *what* would be waiting.

I got out first, then took Chok-Do's hand as he slid out.

My mother stepped out of the car, took another deep

breath, smiled bravely, saying, as if the boy could hear, "This is your new home, Chok-Do."

Maybe a temporary one, I thought. Overnight. Then good-bye, back to Seoul.

My father came around the hood of the car, key in hand, and opened the kitchen door.

Within a second, two huge animals appeared on the threshold, staring out, wagging their tails. One of them had eyes the color of a steamed oyster.

Chok-Do panicked, a high-pitched screech coming from him, and he took off down the driveway, running as fast as his little legs could carry him, the "eeeeee" sound following him like the tail of a kite.

Startled, none of us reacted until Daddy yelled, "Luke, go catch him."

Luke was just a step ahead of me as we went after Chok-Do, grabbing him before he reached the intersection of Denham.

6

Chok-Do began to cry almost the moment that Luke grabbed him and I was surprised. I thought mutes could make no sounds. Now, Luke was carrying him and the tears were falling. And he'd also made that chilling "eeeeee" when he saw Tuck and Daisy. He was not soundless.

My father and mother were out in the front yard by now and she took Chok-Do into her arms, consoling him.

What a way to be greeted to the U.S.A., and I thought the first thing to do was introduce him properly to Tuck and Daisy. If we kept him, he would have to live with them. There was no way we'd send those two dogs off to another home, whether Chok-Do was frightened or not. If that were the case, I'd go too.

Daddy suggested, "I think we have to pretend that he

does hear. Speak to him. I'm sure that's what they did in Korea."

Almost as soon as he was inside the house, I said to him, "You have to meet Tuck and Daisy. They're very nice dogs. They won't hurt you."

Red-eyed, his small face was a blank.

They were sitting side by side in the middle of the kitchen, Daisy gazing at the newcomer, Tuck's dead eyes following the sounds of voices, as usual. His head moved from voice to voice.

Chok-Do was half-hiding behind my mother's legs and she said, "I want to show him around the house, his room and the bathroom . . ."

I said, "He has to meet the dogs first. So he won't be afraid of them." They were always Priority One to me.

Daddy said, "Helen's right."

So I went over and took Chok-Do's hand and led him up to Tuck and Daisy. He held me tightly as I made the proper introductions, touching his hand to their heads while they sniffed. Tuck sniffed him toe to head, getting an indication of his size, then finally blessed him with a wet lick. I think Tuck immediately sensed that something was wrong with this little speechless boy and I knew that Chok-Do realized Tuck was handicapped too. He stared at the gooshie gray eyes.

I could feel the tension go out of his small body and saw half a smile, the round lemon-pie face turning up to look at us, then turning back toward the dogs. It usually worked. Dogs and children.

Soon, we went on the house tour, Tuck and Daisy, never to be left out, padding along behind. Chok-Do was shown his room. New toys and a tricycle told him that's where he belonged. Temporarily, at least.

Our two-story white clapboard house hasn't changed very much since I was born. Thankfully, my mother has left my bedroom much as it was when I occupied it permanently from kindergarten through high school, except for a period in which Chok-Do resided in there.

Up the stairs, turn sharp left and go down the hall to the end, past Luke and Stan's room, and there I was, there he was, opposite my parents' bedroom. I forgot those two bathrooms along that hall, each with claw-footed tubs. Nine-eleven West Cheltenham was built in the 1920s.

Downstairs hasn't changed that much, either. Some fresh paint a while back; a few more books in the den. The living room, with its wide smoke-stained fireplace, hasn't changed at all. Maybe the big overstuffed chairs and the sofa are showing wear that I hadn't noticed before. Who's to worry? It's a lived-in, homey house, a house of warmth.

The dining room is the same: huge, round oak table in the middle, under the Tiffany chandelier, and a big oak buffet with a mirror over against the far wall. There are a few more cracks in the green kitchen tile, near the sink, but my mother laughs, saying, "Everything ages."

So it does but I think our old house is doing it gracefully. The outside is exactly the same as it was in 1958.

My parents had had fun buying toys for a six-year-old and making a sign in Korean that said, "Welcome, Chok-Do," and now, standing outside my former—now his—room, watching him as he looked in, my mother was saying, "We're trapping ourselves."

"I know," Daddy said.

So did I.

If we gave him up, sent him "home," how could we explain it to him? Tell him we didn't want him because he was deaf? There was no way to tell him that, explain anything, say, "We're sorry but . . ." No way at all. No way.

He turned and looked at us, then edged into the room, examining the toys, including the shiny new tricycle. He rested the koala, stroked the new chrome handlebars and ran a small hand over the trike's black seat, finally looking up at us in wonderment as if to say, "Is this all for me?"

Tuck and Daisy brushed past us. That room was their home too.

No way to tell him.

I said, "Do you think he knows sign language?"

Luke scoffed, "He's too young to know anything."

My mother said, "I'm not sure of that. He seems very intelligent."

Watching him inside the room—we were all standing outside as if we were observing a monkey in the zoo—Daddy said, "I wonder if they teach sign language in Korea?"

His hands were running over the trike again.

Mother said, "I've got a whole lot of questions to ask."

I said, "Is sign language the same here as it is over there?"

Mother said, "I haven't the faintest."

My father shrugged.

Luke said, "You mean we've got to learn *their* sign language?" Before anybody could answer, he added, "If we keep him."

Mother frowned, saying, "Ssshhh . . ."

Daddy snorted, "Even if he could hear, I doubt he'd understand English."

By that time, Chok-Do was on his hands and knees, playing with a windup truck, lost in a child's world. All eyes were still on him.

"Luke, go bring his bags up," said Daddy.

"Stay with him, Helen," said my mother. "I have to fix lunch."

It was that time of day.

Excitement, for them, temporarily over, Tuck and Daisy were stretched out on the carpet, already asleep. They'd taken Chok-Do in stride. No problem for them, as of now.

I sat down on the floor near him again, thinking that it was going to be awfully difficult for my parents to send him away, deaf and speechless or not. All the papers had been signed, to my knowledge. Less than two hours had passed and it wasn't a matter of official papers now. It was a problem of heart.

.   .   .

At lunch, he ate his tuna sandwich without once looking at any of us. His eyes were directed either toward his plate or toward Tuck and Daisy. He'd already developed a kinship with them, I thought. He could only make sounds. They couldn't speak either. Perhaps he'd been around a dog in that village outside Seoul.

I said, "Do you think he knows they fooled us?"

Daddy said, "Fooled us?"

"Sent him over without saying what was wrong with him? The adoption people over there."

"They had to know," my mother said. "He doesn't know but *they* had to know. If only they'd been honest."

Luke said, "If they had, you wouldn't have signed the papers."

There was a silence, then Daddy said, glancing over, "I guess not."

My mother looked over at him, studied him a moment, then nodded her agreement. Frowning, she said, "If we both didn't work . . ."

They were already looking for a way out, I thought. An excuse.

That wasn't like us, the tough Ogdens.

Luke said, "Well, what do we do? Turn him over to the state?" That was Luke, right to the sharp point.

Mother closed her eyes. "Please don't ask that kind of question. Not now, not yet."

7

I tried to imagine what it would be like to live in Chok-Do's world without sound, see all the mouths moving, not knowing what they were saying, see cars move and not hear the engines, not hear the wind, the drip of rain. No music, no church bells. Everywhere there was sound, even in most silent places, and he heard nothing. Nothing.

I asked Tuck if blindness was worse than deafness. He snored on.

Stan arrived home from the Safeway about five-fifteen, grocery-bagging done for the day, and I could hear his shout from the kitchen, "Where is everybody?"

I yelled from my "old" room. "Up here!"

Tired from the long flight, Chok-Do had slept awhile after lunch but was now playing with his new toys, and I'd been assigned again to keep watch, along with the dogs. Be big sister. Frankly, baby-sit! What else could you call it? Luke was smart. He took off without saying where he was going.

Stan, tall and good-looking—Luke and Stan got all the good Ogden genes—came into the room and said to the Korean boy, "Hey, I'm Stan, your new brother," and started to walk over to him.

Tuck and Daisy got up and wagged their tails.

I said, "Stan, he can't hear or speak."

Stan pulled up, gasping, "What?" echoing Father at the airport.

"He's a deaf-mute."

"I don't believe it," said Stan, walking on over to Chok-Do, who was now assembling a Tinkertoy.

He repeated, "I'm Stan, your new brother."

There was no reaction, of course. Chok-Do had no way of knowing that Stan was behind him, three feet away.

Frowning widely, shaking his head, Stan looked at me. "Good Lord, what are we going to do? Why didn't they tell us?"

I couldn't answer either question and shook my own head.

"Where's Mom, Dad?"

"At the library."

"At the library? On Saturday afternoon?"

"Trying to find a book on the deaf. Dad's idea."

I thought it was a good one.

"Oh," said Stan, looking again at the back of Chok-Do's round crew-cut head, still frowning.

I said, "I'll try to introduce you," and got off the bed, going over to Chok-Do, tapping him on the shoulder, pointing to Stan, then pointing to myself. I was using sign language without even knowing it. I said, "This is Stan, my oldest brother."

The big eyes studied Stan, who bent down and extended his hand. Chok-Do took it briefly in a shake, then returned to making the Tinkertoy windmill.

"Some impression I made," said Stan.

"What did you expect?" I said.

Back on the bed, both of us sitting on the edge, Stan asked, "How did Mom take it?"

"Fell apart at first but you know her."

"Are we going to keep him?" There was that awful question again.

"I don't think they know what to do."

Sitting there, watching him, all sorts of questions had bobbed through my mind: How could he go to a regular school? Who could he play with? Could he have an operation that might help him? A hearing aid? Was he stone-deaf?

After a thoughtful silence, Stan said, "I think they should send him back before they get attached to him."

I said, "They? It's all of us."

Stan said, "Why didn't they just refuse him at the airport?"

"There was no chance. There he was. We'd already met him when we found out he was deaf."

Stan sighed and shook his head again. "The people over there had to know it."

That didn't alter the fact that he was here on Cheltenham, adoption papers signed and sealed. "Dad said they'll find out more tomorrow or Monday."

Stan shook his head. "Blind dog, deaf boy, what's this family coming to?"

I certainly didn't have an answer.

Stan rose up, saying he had to take a shower; he was going out on a date. Coward.

I rose up too, taking Chok-Do by the hand, telling the dogs it was time for the evening walk. Twice daily I took them to the park, my training ground for the famous team of Tuck and Daisy.

On the way to the park I stopped by Ledbetter's to introduce Chok-Do to Mr. Ishihara. He grinned widely at the Korean boy and shook his hand but the grin vanished when I told him that Chok-Do was stone-deaf.

"Oh, no," said Mr. Ishihara, alarmed.

I said it was true.

"They didn't tell you."

"Not a word. I'm not sure we'll keep him."

"I'm so sorry for you both," Mr. Ishihara said, frown of concern on his smooth face.

"I know," I said, and headed on for the park. Once there, Tuck followed the ring of Daisy's bell as they sniffed and ran around, as usual.

Chok-Do, who had trudged along beside me, as obedient as Tuck and Daisy, immediately went to the swings and sat down in one. Swings are universal. As I shoved him, he made a sound. It wasn't that "eeeeee" of terror when he first saw the dogs. It was a different sound, an "aaaaah," a sound that might mean joy.

I finally got him up as high as the swing would go and suddenly I heard laughter. I looked around but no other children were on the swings. So it had to be coming from Chok-Do. I stepped to the side to look at him, and yes, he was laughing. So the speechless deaf could laugh as well as cry.

He knew how to pump so I let him do that for a while, then whistled for the dogs. They came running and we headed back toward home in the twilight. I said to Chok-Do, "You like that, huh?" without thinking he couldn't respond. He didn't look up. So I stopped and turned him so that he was facing me, doing a swing gesture with my hands.

He laughed and nodded.

Maybe we *could* communicate, after all, I thought. With our hands and eyes.

Just after we crossed Denham, I saw him looking straight up. I looked up too. A four-engined aircraft, a Connie, was passing overhead.

Chok-Do *could* hear. He wasn't stone-deaf.

Excited about my discoveries, as soon as I got into the house, I said, "He can laugh and he can hear airplanes."

My father said, "Helen, all deaf people can cry or laugh except those who don't have vocal cords or tongues. And I don't think Chok-Do heard any airplane. He felt the vibrations."

"How do you know that?"

"I've lived longer than you have."

To make him feel at home, Mother had fixed *pul-go-gi*—beef strips marinated in soy sauce, sesame oil, toasted sesame seeds and other things—and we'd barbecued them on the grill. We ate outside on the back patio and again he kept his head down, not looking at any of us.

Usually, there was a lot of talk at our dinner table but this evening a shadow was cast over it. Four of us could hear and talk; one couldn't. What little conversation there was seemed strained. My mother noticed it and said, "We're making him feel like a stranger."

That was a silly thing to say. He *was* a stranger. But we all knew what she meant.

Then, suddenly, I knew again what the shadow really was; I think we all did. The daylong shadow was that big decision: was Chok-Do to stay with the family or go back to Korea?

After dinner we watched TV in the den. Saturday nights back then never offered much but he sat there, stroking the dogs in front of the black-and-white, eyes glued on "The Grand Ole Opry." There was a choice of the Nashville hillbillies, a game show, wrestling or a Western movie. Those were the gentle days of "Davy Crockett," of "Lassie" and "Leave It to Beaver." In the morning he could have cartoons, I thought.

After a while he yawned and Mother said, "Let's get him up to bed."

Having lived in a church orphanage most of his life, Chok-Do was far from helpless, we discovered, and he took his single pair of pajamas out of the drawer and we left the room as he changed. Then he marched out to the bathroom, toothbrush and Korean toothpaste in hand.

Mother said, "He has a lot of independence. That's good."

I thought so too. He might need it.

The basin was old-fashioned and high, with big porcelain handles on the faucets. His arms were too short to reach the water taps and I crossed to my room to get a chair. "What about that little stool I used to use?" I said.

"It's in the garage loft. We'll get it in the morning."

Tuck and Daisy had come upstairs and had settled down in one of their usual spots, eyeing the activity.

The koala was already placed on the edge of his pillow.

I said, "That's the dirtiest bear I've ever seen." It was shiny slick from handling. Grimy, even.

Mother said, "I'm sure you know koalas aren't bears. They're marsupials." Always the teacher.

"It should be dry-cleaned," I said.

"Heaven forbid," she said.

Bathroom routines over, Chok-Do came straight back to "his" room and knelt down by the bed, his hands folded.

Was he praying? We couldn't see his lips.

But if he was praying, *how did he know to do it?* What to say to God?

If he was deaf, how could he have been taught to pray?

My mother put her hand to her mouth.

I stood there thinking it might be a long, painful day before we sent Chok-Do back to that orphanage.

A few minutes later, we tucked him in and turned the light off. He was clutching the koala. We weren't fifteen feet down the hall before the light came back on.

My mother said, "Hmn," and reversed course.

Mother went over to the bed lamp and turned it off and the same thing happened again. Determined kid.

This time, she said, "Maybe he slept with the lights on in Korea," and we continued downstairs.

Sometime after we all went to bed he got up and put himself and his pillow between the two dogs, the position in which my father found him the next morning. Tuck and Daisy didn't care.

After breakfast I turned on the TV and he laughed loudly at the antics of "The Road Runner."

I sat down on the big braided, oval rag rug near him. In a moment, he ootched over and took my hand. I think my love affair with little Chok-Do began that Sunday morning. I could now become Big Sis, good for my ego.

8

After meeting my new brother, Mrs. Gaines, a buxom woman who looked to be in her fifties, beginning to gray, said, "I'm as shocked as you are. I had no idea."

Except Stan, who was again bagging groceries, all the Ogdens, including Tuck and Daisy, were in the living room. "I'll find out but it's 4 A.M. Monday over there. I'll call later today." It was still Sunday over here.

"Why would they do it?" my mother asked.

"I'm sure you've guessed. They wanted better medical care, a better education for him. They haven't done this too often but they've done it. They gamble that the adoptive parents will go along with one defect or another."

"Have they?" Daddy asked.

"The adoptive parents? Yes. I recall only two children being sent back. They were older. It was difficult for everyone. It's always best to go over there and see the child yourself."

"But you said that Chok-Do was from a very remote village and wouldn't be brought to Seoul until the last minute," said my mother.

"Obviously, they weren't being truthful. I feel very badly about this for you, and for him."

Chok-Do was down on the floor, rubbing along Tuck's back, very much to the dog's approval. He was paying no attention to any of us. Already they were a team.

"What are our alternatives?" Daddy asked.

"Well, though it's not written down exactly that way, you have six months before the adoption is final and you can opt out. But I'd urge you to do it tomorrow if you decide you don't want to go through with it. Otherwise, you might become too attached to him. He, to you."

"Tomorrow?" my father said, a troubled look on his face.

Mrs. Gaines nodded. "Then we'll immediately try to place him with another family. In the meantime, he'll be a ward of the state. After six months or so, if we can't find a permanent family for him we'll return him to Seoul."

I said, "Why can't we try the six months?" I was on his side.

Looking over at me, distressed, Mother said, "Helen, we've got to think about it and talk about it. We can't make that decision this morning."

"Making him a ward of the state will be like putting him back into an orphanage over here," said my father, frown widening.

Mrs. Gaines nodded. "Exactly. It will be a place for handicapped children run by the state."

I said, "Don't do that to him. Please don't."

"Helen! . . ." There was sharp annoyance in my mother's voice, anger in her eyes.

Mrs. Gaines said, "Another alternative is to go through with the adoption and place him in the School for the Deaf at Riverside. You'll see him weekends, holidays, in the summer . . ."

"That's not like having our own child here in the home," said my father, even more dismayed.

"There's no ideal solution to this, Mr. Ogden. But please don't have any guilt feelings no matter what you do."

"How can we not have guilt feelings?" said my mother, with a low, brittle laugh. "How can we not?"

"None of this is your fault, just like Chok-Do's deafness is not his fault." She nodded to Tuck. "He didn't wish blindness on himself, did he?"

I answered that one strongly. "No, he didn't."

"The fault here lies with the church adoption agency in Seoul. He's an attractive child, he's probably bright, and they took the risk you'd keep him, as I said."

"I think he can hear a little," I said.

Luke got into it. "What do you know, Helen?"

"I had him out yesterday afternoon, remember?" I said.

Daddy said, sharply, "That's enough, both of you."

"Suppose we all learned sign language?" said my mother, grasping at any solution.

Mrs. Gaines looked over. "That's quite an undertaking, I'd guess. But that's also another alternative, I guess. The trouble is that he'd lack playmates his own age. Again, there's no ideal solution."

"What is there besides sign language?" Daddy asked.

Mrs. Gaines shook her head. "I don't know anything about training for the deaf except that the emphasis is now on oral communication. Teaching him to speak. The experts are dead against sign language, I've heard."

Silence fell over the room again and Mrs. Gaines finally broke it. "Think about it, talk about it, and call me as soon as possible."

She knelt down by Chok-Do, hugged him, kissed him and said good-bye to all of us.

Openly rooting for Chok-Do now, I said, "I'm already doing sign language with him."

Mother said, looking exasperated, "Helen, please. We're all trying to talk with our hands but pointing to your open mouth to ask him if he's hungry isn't sign language."

I disagreed. "Okay, why can't we all learn the real sign language?"

Mother said, "You heard Mrs. Gaines."

Luke said, "I have enough problems learning my own language."

"Yes, you do," Mother agreed.

That afternoon I spent some time with Chok-Do in his room, playing a game with him that didn't require speech. Tuck and Daisy were there, as usual, and at one point he looked over at them and said what sounded like "woof-woof."

I'm sure he said it. He knew what they were.

Looking straight at him, I said, "Say that again, Chok-Do."

His face went back to a complete blank.

I went down to the yard, where my mother was cultivating the impatiens. I said, "Chok-Do just talked."

She sat back on her haunches. "What?" She dropped her three-pronged digger and put her hand flat to the top of her head, a familiar gesture.

"He just talked."

"What did he say?"

"Woof-woof."

My mother laughed helplessly. "Helen, for pete's sakes, that isn't a word. That's like him saying 'rye' or 'ooooo.' "

I insisted, "Mother, he looked at Tuck and said, 'Woof-woof' . . ."

She shook her head. "I hope we don't all go crazy. He doesn't know a dog's bark. He can't know it because he can't hear it. He doesn't even know what to call the animal."

I stormed, "You don't want to listen," and ran back into the house.

. . .

Sunday night we had soup for dinner and Chok-Do didn't use the soup spoon. He picked up the bowl and drank from it, making a lot of slurping noises.

Stan said to him, "Hey, you're supposed to use a spoon."

Mother said, "Not in Korea."

"This is the U.S.A.," Stan said. "He's got to learn. Making all that noise."

Daddy said, patiently, "Stanley, he can't *hear* himself slurping."

Stan looked embarrassed and said, "I'm sorry."

We were learning.

The slurping continued as talk died away.

I finally said, "I was thinking this afternoon about the things we can do with him."

Looking over, Daddy asked, "What things?"

"Things that don't require hearing. Kid things. Disneyland and the rides. The San Diego Zoo and Sea World. He doesn't need to hear to enjoy the rides or look at the animals."

My mother nodded. "And we just get deeper and deeper."

Daddy observed, "We're in pretty far already."

Slurp! Slurp!

Just before bed that night, Luke and I caught him talking to the dogs. He'd gotten into his pajamas on his own and was sitting on the floor in his room, Tuck and Daisy down on their bellies looking at him as though they were listening. His back was to us.

"Awk . . . eeek . . . rye . . . fum . . . rye . . . eerk . . ."

Luke laughed and said, "He sounds like a constipated pig."

"You've never heard a pig talk," I said.

"He's not making any sense, Helen. Oink-oink."

I didn't think he was, either, but wouldn't admit it. "Makes sense to him."

Then Chok got up on his knees and hugged Tuck and Daisy.

Luke shook his head and went on down to his new room, where Stan was trying to sleep. One of those "doozies" of a fight had already occurred over the radio, when and who could play it.

Mother came up and we "put" Chok-Do to bed, kneeling down with him as he said his "prayers" or whatever they were.

9

Next day, taking Tuck and Daisy, I went to Mr. Ishihara to tell him how disappointed I was with my parents; that they were actually considering giving up Chok-Do.

Looking at me gravely, speaking slowly, he said, "I'm sure this is a terrible struggle for them. If they adopt him, they—*not you*—are responsible for him. Maybe for a long, long time. They have to find a way to educate him, take care of his health, do everything for him that they've done for you."

"But they could at least try."

"Knowing them, I think they are trying."

Oh, I knew they were. I understood some of the reasons. Mother would be going back to teaching the day after Labor Day. There was no special school for Chok-Do closer than Riverside. No playmates. Yet . . .

"What do you know about sign language?" I asked.

Mr. Ishihara said he knew nothing about it. He'd only seen deaf people use it.

I said we'd been told that the experts were against sign language.

He said, "A lot of people with good hearing talk with their hands. You ever seen the Italians talk? Their hands are flying." Mr. Ishihara was always positive. He added, "Experts are often wrong about things."

That's what I thought too.

"But you'll have to teach him as well as yourself."

"I can try," I said. I'd done it with Tuck, hadn't I? Taught him about guiding, the most difficult thing I'd ever done.

Mr. Ishihara grinned at last. "That's the way."

So I went from Ledbetter's to the Montclair Library, parking Daisy and Tuck out by the steps, and found a book entitled *Signing for the Deaf.* In it were hand diagrams for words. How to hold the hands and fingers, and *talk.*

There were drawings of objects and then, below them, the right sign. I thought Chok-Do might recognize them. There were all kinds of categories and the finger signs for them: *Heart*—trace a heart on the chest with the index finger.

There was an alphabet for finger spelling: *A* was a closed fist with the thumb sticking up; *B* was four fingers sticking up, thumb across the hand.

Excited, I practically ran home clutching *Signing for the Deaf* and went into the house on a trot, calling for my mother.

She was upstairs with Chok-Do and I took the steps

two at a time and ran on into his room, where she was sitting on the bed, watching him. His back was to us.

"Look what I've got," I said, showing her the book, which was about half as thick as a Sears catalog, and the same size.

She looked at it silently.

"Now we can all learn sign language," I said.

After turning a dozen pages, she put the book down on her lap and said, pointedly, "You notice he didn't even hear you come into the room."

What did that have to do with the sign-language book? Of course, he couldn't hear me.

She said, "Helen, I think it's wonderful that you're doing this but the problem is much greater than us learning sign language—if we ever could. The problem is trying to figure out what's best for him over the next fifteen or twenty years. That's the problem. We could harm him rather than help him. Try to understand."

There was that word again. *Try*. Try.

I said, "Well, why can't we all *try* to learn how to talk to him with our hands?"

She took a deep breath. "We can," she said, low and lifeless, surrendering.

I noticed that in only four days her face had a tiredness to it that I'd never seen before. There were signs of darkness beneath her eyes. She wasn't sleeping well.

I looked over at Chok-Do. He didn't even know I was there.

I went over to him, sat down beside him, opened the book so that he could see the diagrams. Then I turned to the index to find the word "teach." The diagram was on page 246: "Place both open 'AND' hands in front of the forehead, facing each other; bring them forward, away from the head, into closed 'AND' positions." The hand positions meant taking something from the mind to pass on to others.

I tapped the diagram and said to Chok-Do, in Pidgin English, my finger pointing *me*, then pointing *you*, "I'm going to teach you."

He just blinked. He didn't understand one thing.

I heard a sound behind me and turned. Tears were coming down my mother's face. She got up and quickly left the room.

Turning to the index again, I looked up "dog," finding it on page 88: "Pat the leg and snap the fingers." I pointed to Tuck, said, "Dog," patted my leg and snapped my fingers.

I did it four or five times. *"Dog! Dog! Dog!"*

Finally Chok-Do pointed at the dog, patted his leg and snapped his fingers.

I hugged him.

His saying "dog" would come later, I knew.

The next morning there was a new development. I went out in the backyard and saw Chok squatting beside Tuck and doing something to the dog's coat. He was so intent he didn't see me. Tuck was on his side on the cool cement of the garden walkway, apparently enjoying what was going on.

Closer, I saw that Chok was searching for fleas and whenever he'd find one he'd use his thumb and forefinger to mash it.

After watching for a moment or two, I went back into the kitchen, believing that there must have been a dog around that Korean orphanage. How else would he have known that dogs have bugs? He'd seen someone else do this.

"I can't think of a better job for him," my mother said, promising not to tell Luke.

Brother Chok, the flea-picker.

Another thing that was evident right away—Chok was an explorer. He'd already checked out every nook and cranny of the old house, opening drawers, closets and cupboards. He was curious about everything and I could only think that the orphanage had been as barren as a military school.

There was absolutely nothing wrong with Chok's mind, that we could tell. During these weeks a car commercial was running on TV, with the bearded salesman, in a Western hat, holding up two fingers on his right hand in a V-for-victory sign. Chok didn't see it more than twice before he was grinning back at the set, holding up a V. Although he had no idea what it meant it became *his* sign.

10

Children's Hospital, a place of both hope and heart-break, is at Sunset and Vermont in Los Angeles. I think Chok-Do knew immediately what it was as soon as we pulled into the parking lot. He saw ambulances with the Red Cross on their sides. His eyes grew wide at the sight of the big building and I thought, for a moment, that he might jump out and run away. He'd been to this kind of place before.

Tuck and Daisy were standing up in the space behind the backseat. I told them we wouldn't be long.

I wasn't all that thrilled about having to go there this third Thursday in June. Hospitals smelled like hospitals and reminded me of sickness. It was a command performance on my part, Mother claiming I needed to come along for hand-holding. Both hers and Chok-Do's, she said.

My father was helping to design a power system for a

Northern California industrial plant and couldn't take time off to be with us.

By this morning Mrs. Gaines had contacted the church people in Seoul and they admitted knowing Chok-Do was deaf but hoped he wouldn't be sent back. Mrs. Gaines had correctly guessed the reasons—better medical care, better education, a good family.

"Have you made a decision?" she asked, on the phone.

My parents had talked a lot about it, my father calling from Stockton every night.

"No," my mother said. "We decided to have him tested."

For better, for worse, over the last six days Chok-Do seemed to have made his own firm decision: the dogs and myself were his family favorites. During his waking hours he tagged along behind me or them. Every time I'd turn around he'd be there, brown eyes aimed at me. Perhaps it was because I was the youngest and because I had charge of Tuck and Daisy. He had all but adopted them. Either reason, it was nice to be loved.

One thing we definitely knew by now, Chok-Do could make many different sounds. They weren't English and they weren't Korean, either. They were gibberish, in my mother's opinion. They were "aaahees" and "ooooos" and "ryes" and "eeks" and "onks" and "eerps" and "awks." They were funny sounds but they were also painful to hear. He "talked" mainly to himself or the dogs.

Soon, we were in a testing room of the Hearing and Speech Clinic, an appointment having been made by our own doctor. He'd examined the new and maybe temporary Ogden member on Monday afternoon, finding him fit in all ways except one—his cocoon of silence.

Chok-Do was looking all around the room and Mother said, "I have an idea he's been through this before." On a table were noisemakers.

"In Korea?"

She nodded.

Two women came in wearing green hospital smocks, the youngest carrying a note-board. The older made the introductions, saying the procedure was quite simple.

Chok-Do would sit in a chair and she'd make various noises behind his back. The young audiologist would take notes on any reactions. She would be facing Chok-Do, along with us.

I guided him into the chair and he sat down, folding his hands.

I looked over at my mother. Her eyes were closed and I knew she was saying a short, quick prayer. Let him hear *something, anything.*

The tester said, "Here we go," and rang a dinner bell behind Chok-Do's head.

His expression didn't change. He didn't hear it.

"Watch his eyes," the tester said. "They're the tell-tales."

For the next half hour, she made noise with all sorts of gadgets that honked and buzzed and clicked, moving them high and low, left and right, behind him.

While this was going on, Chok-Do fidgeted and

looked around the room, stared at me, swung his legs, fiddled with his hands, scratched his scalp.

But there wasn't even the tiniest flicker in his eyes as a whistle was blown sharply behind his head. "Anything?" the older technician asked the younger one, who'd been writing steadily.

A slow shake of head was the answer.

My mother was devastated. I felt very sad.

Then we took him to an ear, nose and throat specialist down the hall who looked at the audiology notes, examined Chok-Do's ears and finally said, "He's profoundly deaf. I'd guess his mother had rubella."

That was measles, I knew.

"What do we do?" my mother asked.

"I understand from Dr. Alexander that this is an adoption case," the doctor said.

Mother nodded.

"If it was me, I'd think twice about going through with it. You'll have a struggle ahead, Mrs. Ogden. Horrendous struggle. You really won't have a child. You'll be lucky if he ever talks. He'll need special schooling . . ."

The brutal truth hurt that morning.

"There's no chance?" Mother said, lips tight.

"Practically none."

"But he makes all those sounds," she said. "Rye, awk, eek . . ."

The doctor nodded. "Deaf children, deaf adults, have some strange vocalizations. You'll be astonished at the volume of sound when this one is really upset over something. A deaf child's tantrum is cyclonic."

I was angry. I said, "I opened the door to his room last night. He turned to look at me. I'm sure he heard me."

The doctor shook his head. "He saw the light change in the room. He didn't hear you at all."

How did the doctor know? He wasn't in the hallway.

I said, "He kneels down and prays every night before going to bed."

The doctor shook his head. "He's aping other children he saw at the orphanage." Like picking fleas?

I said, "He laughs at TV cartoons."

"Okay. But don't you realize he can't hear himself laugh."

I hadn't thought about that. It silenced me.

"If he wants more milk he can't ask for it. He'll have to go get it," the doctor said.

Okay, I thought. So he has to get it. Big deal.

"Will you get angry at him for leaving the water faucets running? He can't hear them."

What he was saying was both for my mother and myself.

"When he's hungry all he can do is point to his stomach," the doctor said.

I stayed shut up.

Mother said, "I took him along to Bullock's Wilshire yesterday afternoon and lost him in housewares. I felt like a fool walking around calling out, 'Chok-Do, Chok-Do.' I finally found him in the toy department down on the next floor. I guess he'd seen it riding up on the escalator. He doesn't seem to be afraid to go off by himself."

The doctor nodded. "You wouldn't believe the ways this child can make your life miserable. Even pure hell. How can you tell him not to play with matches, that he might set the house on fire? The only real way he can learn is to burn himself."

She was silent a moment, despair on her face, then asked, "What about all of us learning sign language?"

The doctor said, "Mrs. Ogden, we frown on sign language, quite frankly. What we strive for is full oral communication, teaching him to talk like a normal person. We're very much against signing . . ."

There it was again.

"Should we investigate the state-run school in Riverside?"

He shrugged. "That's pretty far from Los Angeles and I hear that freeway won't be ready for a while yet."

"Well, what should *we do*?"

"I'd suggest you take him to the John Tracy Clinic in Beverly Hills. They deal in the baby to six-year-old range. Have him tested again there, see what they recommend."

My mother, a little numb by this time, thanked the doctor and we departed the clinic.

We went back out to the parking lot and Chok-Do climbed into the rear end of the station wagon, dog territory, hugging them, ruffling their coats. His way of speaking the "ryes" and "awks" certainly didn't bother them. They enjoyed the new language.

What the doctor said about him not being able to hear himself laugh was the worst of all, I guess.

11

There are several kinds of dog stealers loose in this country of ours, the worst kind being those who see a good one on the streets and kidnap it in broad daylight, take it miles away from home and a broken-hearted family.

Another kind is the "inside" thief who steals the dog out from under the legal owner's nose at home. That can happen to a daughter or son if the father, for instance, comes along and begins wooing the dog, being real friendly to it, playing with it, taking it out for romps. Little by little, the dog transfers allegiance.

In the human world, that is known as "alienation of affection" and can result in a lawsuit. I could not sue Chok-Do but little by little he was surely stealing Tuck and Daisy away from me.

They no longer slept by my bed, seldom even came into my new room and even seemed to wag their tails less when I approached. I admit it bothered me somewhat but I thought it would wear off. I tried to think of it as Chok-Do being a new toy for them to play with.

When he went upstairs, they followed; when he came down, they were right behind him. Likewise, they trooped into the backyard whenever he went out there. If I called to them, it almost seemed that they checked with him before answering me. This was all happening within a matter of two weeks, and my resentment was building, much as I fought it.

I couldn't figure it out except to think that the dogs were a lot more fickle than I'd ever realized. Their true love for me wasn't as true as I'd always thought.

A little after two, Friday, Steffie's mother called out to the pool from their kitchen window. "Your mom's on the phone," she said.

I got out of the water, dried off and went inside.

Mother's voice was urgent when she asked, "Is Chok-Do with you?"

I said he wasn't. He was napping when I left the house. Or I thought he was. He was on his bed.

"Are Tuck and Daisy with you?"

"No." I sometimes took them to Steff's house but not this day.

Mother said, "Well, I think they're with Chok-Do. You have any idea where they might have gone?"

He had my dogs? My dogs! That was incredible.

"To the park, maybe." He'd come along with me on the dog walks, morning and afternoon, since arriving, and I'd always taken them on their usual routes to the park and to Ledbetter's. No other places I could think of.

"You better come home and help me find them." There was a pause. "No, meet me in the park."

The park was about six blocks from Steff's house and we dressed hurriedly, Steff asking, "Has he done this before?" Chok-Do, she meant.

"No," I said, more angry at him than worried about him. Dumb kid. If he was with Tuck and Daisy, he was safe enough. But I was bothered by the fact that he took them and they were dumb enough to go along with him. Was I losing all control over them?

"Tuck can live through anything," Steff said emphatically.

I wasn't sure about that but I knew what Steff meant. He did seem indestructible.

Yet I'd always known, deep down, that a speeding car on West Cheltenham or Denham could kill him; knew that bullets or knives could kill him; bears or mountain lions on our camping trips; even a nasty virus.

"Dumb dogs," I said, also suddenly angry at Tuck and Daisy.

I told Steff that Chok-Do had been paying a lot of attention to them, sleeping with them, rubbing them, talking to them, even picking fleas off them.

"I thought he couldn't talk."

"Making crazy sounds. How would they know the difference?"

We ran most of the way to the park and I found my mother by the fountain that's in the upper corner. "I don't think they're here," she said. "I've looked everywhere. I've asked people. Now, where have you taken Chok-Do before?"

"Only here and Ledbetter's."

"Down Denham?"

I nodded.

Mother said, "All right, I'm going to walk around here once more and you two go to Ledbetter's. If he's there, bring him here." The park is about twenty acres, with lots of trees.

Steff and I ran to the grocery store to find that Mr. Ishihara was in the back room washing carrots. Steff and I were panting as I asked him if he'd seen the Korean boy and the dogs.

"They haven't been here," he said, alarm clearly on his face.

I said, "Well, if they come here, make them stay and call us, please." He said he would.

We ran back to the park and located my mother, who said she was going home to phone the police. "You two start circling all the blocks in the neighborhood."

Where could he have gone? As we half-walked, half-ran, I tried to think of other places he might go. None came to mind.

Steff said, "He's got a lot of guts for a six-year-old."

Yes, he had, especially for one who couldn't hear or speak. "More guts than brains," I agreed.

By four o'clock we'd gone all the way around ten or eleven blocks, asking anyone who was walking or out working on their lawns. No trace of them, a six-year-old and two canines. It was a repeat of that day in March when Tuck had decided to take a hike.

Finally, I said, "I'm going to call home."

We were both tired and footsore. "I hope," said Steff.

There's an apartment building at the corner of Grayson and Catalina and I used the security guard's phone to dial Cheltenham.

I said, "We haven't found them."

Mother thought a moment and then said, "Come on back. The police can cover more ground than you can."

So we started home.

Twenty minutes later, I saw my mother standing on our front porch and as we went up the walk she said, with relief, "They found him."

"Where?" I asked, reaching the steps.

"About three miles up Denham."

I was shocked.

"Three miles," Steff repeated.

"He's all right?" I said.

"I guess so," Mother said, giving me her "miffed-relieved" look.

"And the dogs?"

"Helen, the dogs are fine."

"Okay. I was just checking."

We all waited on the steps until the black and white car pulled up in front. I could see Daisy's big head in the rear-door window. Then an officer climbed out and opened the back door, letting the dogs jump out and reaching in to retrieve Chok-Do.

My mother went down the walk to collect her "temporary son" and thank the police while I was scolding Tuck and Daisy.

One cop looked at Tuck and said, "When I was a boy I had a one-eyed dog named Bonkers."

My mother nodded. "This one is a little nuts too."

I had to agree.

Then she did her own scolding. Even if Chok-Do didn't understand sign language, her shaking finger, directed at him, and the movements of her mouth should have told him to never go off again. Har-de-har.

He was blinking as she led him inside the house.

Saturday morning there was another Oriental crisis.

I'd been with my father a month earlier when he bought the red and white tricycle for Chok-Do, sized for four- to seven-year-olds. He'd ridden it almost every day, up and down the concrete driveway, which was about sixty feet long, ending at the garage, which was separate from the house.

My mother had set limits for him. "Stop here," she said, pointing to where the driveway joined the side-walk; then she walked him back up to the garage door. "Understand, Chok-Do, here to there," she said, point-ing again. "You must not go out into the street, not even on the sidewalk." Those instructions would be the same for a hearing child. Holding the handlebars, she walked the limits with him several times.

She thought he understood.

Then he pedaled soundlessly, the fun of riding the lit-tle trike all over his face. A black-bulb horn was on the handlebars and I squeezed it for him, not thinking that was senseless. All of us were doing that kind of thing all the time, forgetting the barrier that clasped him.

One of us usually kept an eye on him as he went back

and forth, but for a while that morning Luke was playing softball, Daddy was at Montclair Hardware buying a Skilsaw blade, my mother was talking to my grandmother in Hickory, North Carolina, and I was busy bathing Tuck and Daisy. Hot summer, it was a time of scratching.

Chok-Do selected these minutes when everyone was occupied to extend his riding range. He went on to the sidewalk, turning right.

About that time I went over to the side of the garage to get the hose and rinse down Lady Daisy, who was standing forlornly out in the grass. Tuck was tied up at the steps.

I glanced down the driveway.

No Chok-Do.

I dropped the hose and began running toward the sidewalk, yelling for him by habit.

As I cleared the corner of the house next door and looked down the block, there he was parked innocently on the sidewalk in front of the Sadolskys' driveway, watching the heavy traffic whiz by Denham.

Yelling "Chok!" I also saw a red Roto-Rooter van beginning to back out to the street.

Running toward it fast as I could, I began screaming, "Stop! Stop!" at the driver, waving my arms.

Looking in his side-view mirror, he couldn't possibly see the tiny figure on the pavement behind him, nor hear me. His radio was playing loud.

I knew I couldn't reach Chok-Do in time when Daisy came bounding up beside me and I yelled at her, "Get him . . ."

Those years of expert training as a guide dog paid off in a split second as she exploded across two lawns and hit Chok-Do with her front paws, shoving him out of the way and clearing the truck herself by not more than two feet.

The trike toppled over, Chok-Do striking his head on the sidewalk, yelling out in pain as the van continued on into the street, radio blaring, driver still unaware of what had happened.

I knelt down beside Chok-Do, untangling him from the trike, picking him up. He was bleeding from the forehead, wailing.

Lady Daisy, still soaped up, padded alongside as if nothing had happened as I began to lead him home, towing the trike with my left hand.

Reaching our yard, I took him on into the house. My mother was off the phone to Hickory by that time and heard the crying, meeting us at the kitchen steps.

She said, "What happened? He fall off the tricycle?"

I said he did. For the moment, I wasn't about to say what had really happened. One more danger Chok-Do faced, we faced.

"Oh, my," she said, despairingly, and took him over to the sink. Looking closely at his forehead, she said, "This may need stitches."

That was a small enough price to pay, though she didn't know it. I didn't tell her about the escape on Sadolskys' driveway for a long time, not wanting it to be on Chok-Do's "record."

12

The bond between Chok-Do and Tuck grew daily.

Watching Chok playing with Tuck in the backyard or out on the driveway—Chok would throw the tennis ball and Tuck would retrieve it by the sound of where it hit—I remembered Dr. Tobin saying that Tuck's hearing cycles were up to quadruple of mine. He had eighty thousand or more, compared with the human twenty.

When they played hide-and-seek Chok never won. Tuck would sniff the air, his body tense, and then would listen, almost as if he could hear Chok breathe, finally locating the hider.

Chok played rough with Tuck the way he always liked it, jerking the big head side to side, wrestling with him on the grass, Tuck growling deep down inside. Unheard, of course, by his strong little opponent.

Watching them play together, I remembered how Tuck's eyes looked before he went blind. They could actually laugh. And even now the blankness had purpose in it as he directed them toward the Korean.

After they'd tussle a moment or two, Tuck would spring up, the mouth instead of the eyes laughing, throat noises anticipating another bout. And if Chok didn't attack, then he'd go after the little boy, grabbing a wrist between his teeth. More, more, he wanted.

Chok had found an old car-wash towel in the garage and they used it for a tug-of-war, as I'd once used a rag, Tuck pulling my very temporary brother all over the yard, the growls sounding scary, but I knew they were in fun. Chok's laughter, along with tears the only pure sounds he made, filled the summer air.

I also noticed that Tuck sensed when Chok came silently into a room; the head would lift and the gray eyes point in Chok's direction. Whether this was by sound or smell I couldn't tell, but the tail would begin to wag like a banner, sure sign that he knew Chok was present.

If Chok happened to "speak," those funny "awks" or "ryes" or "erks," Tuck would rise, waiting for the touch of a small hand.

If Chok laughed while in front of TV cartoons, I could swear those gooshie gray eyes lighted up, Tuck pleased to hear that sound.

Then there were moments when I saw Chok studying the yellow dog, Tuck seeming to respond as if some mysterious communication were passing between them. They loved each other.

I thought about all that and wondered if there was a

way for Tuck, with his super-sensitive hearing, to serve as Chok's "ears."

Or was this just another example of a Helen Goggle-Eyes fantasy? I wondered, I wondered.

The next day, I said, "Tuck and I will be his ears."

My mother glanced over. "What?"

"We'll do the listening for him."

"Oh, my," she said. "Now, just how will you do that?"

"I'm not sure. But I have good hearing and Tuck can hear a feather drop."

"Helen, I'm willing to try anything but what you've just said doesn't seem possible."

"Daisy has become Tuck's eyes, and so Tuck and I will be Chok's ears."

She just shook her head.

Okay, I didn't know how we'd do it, either.

The next day I asked Mr. Ishihara how to go about it. He scratched his head and said the idea would require a lot of thought, an awful lot.

13

On Wednesday at the John Tracy Clinic, in Beverly Hills, there were short bursts of sound over the control-room speaker, a single tone, louder each time. But nothing registered. Chok sat there like a small Buddha, Band-Aid on his forehead, six stitches beneath it.

At the end of testing, I remember the audiologist told my mother, "Even the most profoundly deaf person has a little hearing. I'd estimate this child's loss is about ninety to a hundred decibels."

"That's a big loss?" my mother asked.

"Very big," was the quick answer.

"Will a hearing aid help at all?"

"It can't hurt," said the audiologist.

A gray test box about the size of a pack of cigarettes, straps attached, was soon brought out, and temporary ear molds were put into place, Chok eyeing them with suspicion.

Then the audiologist began saying, "Bub, bub, bub, bub, bub," increasing the volume as he spoke.

When the "bubs" were at their highest level, Chok blinked and his eyes narrowed.

"He's hearing a faint sound," said the audiologist.

Mother said, "Oh, thank God," and I echoed her silently.

"But I don't think it's enough for him to distinguish words. I could be wrong."

Hopes fell again.

We went away from the Tracy Clinic with a correspondence course on how to teach Chok-Do to talk. It would take years, the Tracy people admitted. They too were against sign language.

Nonetheless, we went to a hearing-aid place and warm plastic was inserted into Chok-Do's ears so that molds could be fitted. He seemed to understand what we were doing and didn't complain. He sat there patiently, looking at me, those glistening brown eyes saying, I hope this is soon over.

The hearing aid was the next to the last step we could take, my mother said. For the moment.

That night we had an earth tremor. I knew it was coming by the way Tuck and Daisy were acting nearing bedtime. They were moving around the hall whimpering, panting.

Los Angeles—in fact, most of Southern California—is undercut with earth faults, the most famous one being the San Andreas. Some people say that one day the Pacific Coast will be at the Arizona and Nevada borders, all of California having fallen into the sea. We who live here scoff at that idea but also know that a big quake, like the one that destroyed San Francisco, will hit sooner or later.

All the known faults had been mapped and Montclair was on one named Toluca. Every so often the earth along Toluca would grind; then we bumped, rattled and rolled. We lived with it, gambling that the big one would be along the San Andreas, further inland.

Chok-Do couldn't have heard the windows and picture frames rattling, the dishes, cups and saucers dancing in the kitchen, but he did feel the vibrations of the quake because he made that chilling "eeeeee" sound again and ran down the hall to jump into bed with me.

He was trembling and I held him tightly, saying to him that everything would be all right. I was hoping my arms would tell him that.

Two days later, he had his first tantrum.

Steff was over. We were downstairs in the kitchen when I heard noises, things being tossed around, then:

"Ryeeeeeeeeeeee."

He sounded like a little banshee and we went running up the steps to find the dogs out in the hall looking into my old room, and inside Chok-Do was storming around.

He'd pulled the covers off the bed and the drawers

from the chest; the closet door was open and some of the things I'd stored in there were on the floor.

The shrill *"ryeeeeeeeee"* continued and I grabbed him, yelling at him, "What's wrong with you?"

He struggled with me, changing the sound to *"Awk-kkkkkkkk,"* his lemon-pie face in a ball of red rage. For his size, he was very strong.

Twisting away from me, he fell on his back and began to kick the floor with his heels.

"What is it?" I yelled at him again, picking him up, shaking him.

"AWKKKKKKKKKK!"

He tried to swat me and I ducked.

Then he began kicking me and I thought, Okay, kid, and slapped him hard.

His eyes grew wide and he collapsed on the pile of bedclothes, angry tears flowing down. He held his palms up and kept crossing his hands over his chest. What was that sign?

The doctor at Children's Hospital had been right. His tantrums were like a hurricane.

"I don't know what he wants," I said to Steff, trying to think what was wrong.

She shook her head helplessly.

I looked around. Something was missing! He'd lost something! That's why he was tearing the room up. There was no use asking him.

I said to Steff, "He's lost something."

"A toy?"

They were scattered all over the place.

"I don't know," I said.

Then I began ticking off the things I'd seen him play with and it finally dawned—maybe his most precious possession of all, the grimy koala.

At the same instant, I almost knew what had happened. Out in the hallway was another kind of thief, one with gooshie gray eyes. Now and then he swiped things and hid them. A shoe, a purse, a tool, anything he could carry in his mouth. This time, a koala, I was betting.

"Stay with him, Steff," I said.

Knowing where most of his hiding places were, I passed Tuck in the hall, saying, "You jerk," and went out into the yard, checking three likely spots with no success. The fourth one, by the corner of my mother's garden shed, produced Chok-Do's treasure, grimier than before.

I shook the dirt off the koala and took it upstairs, handing it over. A wan smile enveloped Chok-Do's stained face as he grabbed it and held it to his chest.

14

My father decided we all needed a break from the constant Chok-Do turmoil, so up we went to my Uncle Ray Johnson's pine-slab cabin in the San Bernardino Mountains. Uncle Ray was my father's half-brother.

Even Stan went along, getting the weekend off from the Safeway. It was Chok's first outing with the family. My mother made certain the koala was packed.

We arrived there Friday about dinnertime, had barbecued ribs and iced tea, then the four of them began playing hearts. Chok-Do and the canines settled down in front of the TV and I went about finishing up a Nancy Drew book I'd brought along.

About nine I took Chok-Do and my four-legged friends out for a pre-bed leg-lifting and squatting session in the woods behind Uncle Ray's. Suddenly they froze and growled, their hackles rising. Chok-Do grabbed my hand.

I looked in the direction their heads were pointing and saw a ball of light bounding through the pines about six feet off the ground. I swear it went right *through* one tree and disappeared. Towing Chok-Do, I took off, sucking wind.

My grandmother Bessie Quick, my mother's mother, had told me about the famous lights of Brown Mountain, back in North Carolina. On a clear night you could see them thirty miles away. But no one lived on Brown Mountain and for years people had gone up there to try and find the lights with no success.

Grammie Bessie had a theory that they were ghost lights leftover from a Cherokee Indian massacre on that mountain in the seventeen hundreds. I doubt there'd ever been a massacre behind Uncle Ray's but I did see clearly that light, as big as a tennis ball.

One evening in Montclair Park, I was going along with Tuck and Daisy by the high hedge of white-blooming oleanders that separate Wickenham Boulevard from the recreation area.

We were about twenty feet from the oleanders when the dogs suddenly stopped and stiffened, fur rising on their backs. They began to growl.

"What's wrong with you?" I asked.

Their eyes were fixed on the oleanders, which looked ghostly enough, anyway, in the twilight.

"What do you see?" I asked.

They kept on growling. Daisy didn't strain on the leash. Neither one would move.

I couldn't see any other dogs, or any animals of any

kind, moving along the hedge. No humans were there, either, unless they were out on the sidewalk, invisible to me through the thick bushes.

I stood a moment, then dropped Daisy's leash, saying, "Okay, go after it," thinking it was a small animal. Maybe a rat.

This was a summer's evening and suddenly a cold breeze seemed to come from the oleanders—yet there was no wind that night at all. It was as if a puff of arctic air had been blown over us.

As soon as the cold puff passed us, the dogs quit growling and their fur went back to normal. I hurried out of the park, convinced they'd seen a ghost, convinced I'd felt one. That was months ago.

Back in Uncle Ray's cabin, I said, "I really saw one this time."

"Saw one what?" my mother asked.

"A ghost. The dogs saw it first. Then I saw it. Chok-Do saw it."

"What did it look like?" my father asked seriously, dumping the queen of spades on Stan at the same time, causing an outcry.

"It looked like a ball of cotton."

"How big?" asked Luke, with a sputtering laugh.

"About the size of a tennis ball."

"Oh, my," said my father.

"She saw what she saw," said my mother, examining her hand.

"Yeah, someone playing tennis in the woods," said Luke, snickering.

Whatever they thought about it, Tuck and Daisy could "see" ghosts and did have a sixth sense. It wasn't just my imagination.

On Sunday, Tuck proved that sixth sense.

About three-thirty, just when we were packing up and getting ready to drive back to Montclair, my mother came in off the porch, asking, "Has anyone seen Chok-Do?"

"He was playing in the yard a while ago," I said. He'd played out there Saturday, yesterday, mostly on the rubber-tire swing that Uncle Ray had rigged up long ago. He'd gone back and forth on that old tire, making his own special noises. Then he'd played in the dirt with a little tin truck. He seemed capable of amusing himself.

The tire was empty, the dusty tin truck was abandoned, we soon saw.

"Oh, no," my mother groaned.

"Let's not panic," said my father. "He's probably wandered back into the woods."

Tuck and Daisy were sleeping on the porch and I awakened them, saying, "Some sitters you are." But how could I expect a blind dog to baby-sit?

Father said, "I'll take the car and go up and down the road, then join you." It was a two-lane mountain blacktop, about a hundred feet from the cabin, but not heavily traveled. "The rest of you split up in the woods."

I said, "I'll take the dogs and go across the road."

"Okay," he said. "But not too deep, Helen. There's a front coming through."

Gray, tumbling summer storm clouds, with lightning flashes, were building far to the east, and the sky over the San Bernardinos was already dark and threatening. The temperature was dropping rapidly.

None of us appeared frightened but we were. It would be a silent search. There was no use yelling for him.

"I'll ask next door," my mother said.

There was a cabin on the other side of Uncle Ray's and wood smoke was coming out of the creek-rock chimney so someone was home. An old man lived there, I knew. We'd said "hello."

Leave it to Luke. He said, "Maybe he got kidnapped."

Mother said, stepping down off the porch, "*Was*, not *got*, and don't start that rumor." Always the teacher.

Stan, Luke and my mother soon headed into the woods behind Uncle Ray's and I crossed the road with Tuck and Lady Daisy to begin the search over there.

I told them what we were doing but they were already exploring, sniffing for their own purposes. All kinds of little animals dwelled in the damp pines. Brown needles littered the ground.

Climbing up to the low ridge, I went about a quarter mile in both directions. There was no sign of him. Just chill mountain silence. No trace of him. So I decided to go back down to the road, see if someone else had found him.

Diagonal from Uncle Ray's, across the blacktop, was a

storm pipe about two and a half feet in diameter. I'd looked up in there once. A tube of solid black was what it was, not very inviting. It dumped drain water into a concrete spillway, then a sluice carried it under the road.

As we passed the mouth of it I noticed that Tuck sniffed and went on by, then turned and went back to sniff again. I said, "Come on, Tuck." Some animal was up in there, I thought. Skunk, raccoon, squirrel, possum. We had better things to do.

But he stayed by the end of the pipe and began to bark, looking at me with those dead-fish eyes. I went over to him, grabbed his collar and tried to tug him away. Eighty pounds of sightless muscle and bone is not easy to move.

Then I thought, *Could it be?* Was Tuck's sixth sense at work? Did he know something I didn't know?

Was Chok-Do up in that steel tube? We'd just happened to pass by it or I never would have even thought of it.

Though useless, I yelled up in the blackness. Again and again.

Then I told Daisy to stay with Tuck and ran across the road to find my parents and brothers, yelling for them. No answer. They'd gone far into the forest.

It had begun to rain, lightly but steadily.

I ran back to the pipe.

Tuck was still barking at whatever was up in there, and the old white-haired man who lived next door hobbled across the road with his cane, saying, "I'll bet that's where he is."

How could Chok be so dumb?

"He might have gone up either part of the Y," the man said. "I saw that darn thing laid. It branches off about a hundred fifty feet up. Don't ask me why."

I said, "Wouldn't he be afraid to go up in there?" That was a stupid question and didn't deserve an answer. Chok-Do Choi wasn't afraid of adventure. He'd try almost anything.

He shrugged. "Kids are funny, you know. If he got himself a flashlight . . ."

I remembered that Uncle Ray always kept a flashlight in the wooden box by the front door.

The rain thickened a little and there was a rumble of thunder as blue lightning zigzagged across the sky. We didn't have many thunderstorms in Southern California, summer or winter, but those that passed by were often severe, causing flash floods. Both Tuck and Daisy had been restless and jumpy in the late morning.

He said, "We're wastin' time, young lady. When this one hits that pipe'll fill with water. That kid'll either be washed out alive or drown up in there."

I looked over toward the woods, hoping and praying I'd see my parents and brothers walking out. Maybe Stan or Luke would volunteer to search the pipe.

The old man said, "I got a strong light over in the cabin. You up to crawlin' a little? You're skinny enough to do it."

Yes, I was, regretfully.

"But I'd hurry if I was you. Rain's gettin' heavier."

What could I say? I nodded. Chok-Do could drown.

"Okay, it's a big boxy red flashlight, just inside my door on a shelf. You can't miss it."

I was back by the pipe in less than two minutes, looking up into that hole, as scared as I'd ever been in my fourteen years on this earth.

"I'll stay right here with the dogs," the old man said. "Your folks ought to be coming back soon."

I nodded.

He said, "Good luck."

I'd need that and more. I nodded again.

I took a deep breath, turned the light on and entered the pipe. There was damp sand in the bottom of it, studded with little rocks, and my hands and knees were already hurting as I moved forward on my belly, my elbows pushing my body along, my head bumping the corrugated top.

I hadn't gone twenty feet when I realized someone else was in the pipe, following me. Turning my head, I shined the light behind me and saw two gooshie gray eyes.

Tuck!

I said, "You go back, right now." The one thing I didn't need up in that tunnel was a blind dog, I immediately thought.

Hunched down, he was staring at me as usual. Dogs can somehow wriggle through the smallest of spaces and he looked at home. I repeated, "Go back," but he was determined to follow me, and the fact that it was tar-black up in there made no difference. That was his world now and following me was what Tuck was all about. My best friend.

I gave up and crawled on, calling out by habit, meeting with dead silence. Maybe he wasn't in the pipe, after all. Maybe he was in the cabin, sitting in front of the TV. And here I was about to get very wet or worse.

It took five or six more minutes to reach the Y, where the pipe branched in two different directions, and I stopped, wondering which route to take: right or left. I took a rock and pounded it on the pipe. My father had said Chok-Do could feel vibrations.

I shined the light up there but saw nothing. The pipe seemed to bend about forty feet ahead.

I pounded again and there was a faint pound in reply. Chok-Do *was* intelligent.

He was up there!

Water had begun to come over the sand, maybe a half-inch deep, and it was constant as I crawled around the bend and finally saw him. In the beam of the old man's light, his dirty face was creased with tears. His shirt and jeans were soiled.

He looked scared. He had every right to be. *So was I.*

I said, "Just listen to me. You'll be okay. But we have to hurry." What good were words? The flow of water was growing steadily.

I could feel Tuck at my heels and thought the best thing to do was to get him turned around and ahead of Chok-Do. He could crawl faster than I could. Tuck could lead him out.

As I reached Chok, I saw Uncle Ray's flashlight on the sand and made a guess that the battery had failed.

I said, "I want you to follow Tuck. Understand? Follow him!" I used sign language.

Chok-Do nodded.

"Now, I'm going to turn him around and both of you

slide by me, and just keep following him. I'll shine the light on you. Understand?"

Eyes wide in his dirty face, he nodded again. Sign language was working. I have to also believe that Friar Tuck Golden Boy knew what was happening, despite his blindness. In the rays of light he was moving resolutely ahead, crawling toward the pipe entrance, and Chok-Do was close behind him, scurrying along.

"Hurry," I yelled, the water now almost six inches deep. "Hurry, hurry!"

Sounds of splashing and harsh breathing filled the oval.

There was no way for me to know that the thunderstorm had broken over the mountains and rain was pouring down outside. Even if I had known, we couldn't have moved any faster.

We passed the Y and, dimly, I could see light ahead, a round hole of it.

"We're almost there," I told Chok-Do, who was eight or ten feet beyond, crawling for his life.

A hundred forty feet more!

Just then I heard a rumble behind me and the pipe seemed to quiver.

No more than ten seconds passed before the wall of icy water hit us, shoving me into Chok-Do. We were whisked down the pipe in a tangle and flew out as if shot from a pressure hose.

All I remember is being banged around the corrugated-steel surface and landing hard on the spillway, grabbed by Ogden hands as the brown water rushed by.

Tuck and Chok-Do had been scooped up as they came out of that cannon.

Needless to say, we didn't go back to Montclair that stormy afternoon. I took a long, hot shower, then got into bed, nursing bruises and scrapes. My father built a big fire and I was royally served dinner on the couch in the living room, along with a bruised Chok-Do, Luke saying he would have gone up the pipe himself if I hadn't beaten him to it. He couldn't stand it that I was the heroine.

I said, "You're too fat," which wasn't true.

Stan said, "You did good, Sis."

As for Friar Tuck Golden Boy, sleeping in front of the fire, he seemed none the worse for his ride down that chute. One thing was certain: there was a little Korean boy who might not be alive if Tuck hadn't stopped by the end of the pipe and barked.

Dogs *are* smarter than we humans ever give them credit for.

15

"Why me? Why not her?" Luke said. He always seemed to be saying that when I was in my early teens.

I stood in silence, not wanting to go to Riverside, either.

Mother answered, "Because I need Helen with me. That's the only reason, and that's the end of it, Luke. You stay here with Chok-Do and the dogs. You don't have to entertain him. Just don't let him wander off." *We'd had our lessons.*

It was a fine early July day and I knew Luke had plans to take the bus to the beach. He went out of the kitchen with a slap at the door frame, mumbling to himself. I didn't blame him.

My mother believed that by taking Chok-Do along with us to the California School for the Deaf, he'd be reminded of the orphanage in Korea, and wonder if we were about to enroll him. Dump him, that's what. His brain worked very well, as we all knew. So she thought it was wise to leave him home. I thought so too.

It took almost three hours to reach Riverside, traveling along the old pre-freeway roads through those small towns that surround Los Angeles.

Children were out in the play area and the sounds drifting over weren't much different than those at a regular school. There were shouts and laughter. Every so often a "rye" or "awk" was heard. I saw that the teacher with them was using sign language. This school didn't frown on it.

"It looks nice," my mother said, hoping, I knew, to convince herself.

I said, "Hmmmmm."

Okay, it looked nice on the outside like most government buildings look. That's the least thing that can be done for the taxpayers. But what about the inside? I was betting it had all the warmth of a barracks. Poor Chok-Do.

I wasn't saying much. I'd already said it. Everyone knew how I felt. If we were going to keep Chok-Do I was all for putting him in a day school, one of those pick-up-and-deliver schools for little kids. He could have speaking playmates.

They kept telling me that he needed special schooling, not the day-care kindergarten kind. And the playmates he'd have wouldn't understand why he couldn't talk, my father said. It might make matters worse.

"I guess it's like a boarding school," my mother said as we parked near the administration office. Only four or five years old, the brick buildings that were scattered over the large green campus looked new. There were wide walkways connecting the buildings, newly planted trees and shrubbery. Everything was trim and orderly.

Up the short steps we went and into the lobby where the receptionist directed us to the superintendent's office, down a long hall.

Mother had already told him on the phone about our "problem" and this visit was to allow her to see the facilities and talk about what Chok-Do's life would be like if we enrolled him; the schooling he'd get, his deaf playmates.

The superintendent said he believed in a combination of oral communication, lip reading and sign language. He said, "I think Chok-Do will always have to do his listening through his eyes."

Not wanting to be in that room, I only half paid attention: they'd test Chok-Do again as if he hadn't been tested all over town; they'd start him at the preschool level. He'd live with two other little boys in a dorm room, eat in the central dining room with his own age group. He'd have outdoor play periods in good weather. He could come "home" weekends if we'd go in and pick him up, spend holidays with us. He'd be less than a part-time Ogden, not a real member of the family. I held my temper.

We toured the dorm he'd live in, saw the dining room, auditorium, library, swimming pool. All of them okay, I guess, if you didn't have a home of your own.

I kept mostly quiet once again on the way back to

Montclair and Mother suddenly flared at me, "What do you want us to do? Send him back to Korea?"

I didn't answer. Not another word was spoken.

My father was home from Stockton for a few days and after dinner we held a family meeting in the living room, Chok-Do having been sent off to bed. Even Stan was in attendance, having postponed a date until the next night.

"Your mother and I will make the final decision but we want your input," said my father. He often used words like "input" and "gauge" and "test-bed" because of his engineering background.

"Why don't we give him to a Korean family?" said Stan. "That way he'd see familiar faces, eat their food, know their customs . . ."

Mother said, "You don't 'give' humans away."

"You know what I mean," said Stan.

"That's a good idea," said Luke. "No one has thought of that."

"Your mother and I have," said my father. "We've talked about it. Finding the right family wouldn't be easy but it's worth considering."

"What we want is the best thing for him, regardless of our feelings," my mother said. She'd finally taken command of herself the past two days.

I couldn't keep quiet any longer. I said, "The *best* for him is to stay right here and all of us learn sign language. Make him a part of this family, not somebody else's family."

Stan shook his head. "Helen, you've got your needle stuck on the sign language thing. Dad hasn't got time to learn it, Mom hasn't got time; I don't."

Luke looked over at me and said, "I don't, either. Only you and that kid have the time."

Mother sighed. "He isn't 'that' kid."

"If we just learned five signs a day," I said. "And he learned that many . . ."

My father sighed. "The idea is great but it would take us ten years . . ."

"They're not that hard," I insisted.

"That just isn't true, Helen," Daddy said. "I've inquired. Even if we had a teacher come in twice a week, you'd be talking about three years just to master some simple sentences. Sure, we could all learn some individual signs but that isn't communication."

I didn't know he'd investigated.

"What he needs is regular schooling and playmates his age," said my mother, looking straight at me. "You can't provide the schooling of children. I can't, either."

"Yeah," said Luke. "He needs to go to school."

My father interrupted, finally, "What we're going to do is send him to Riverside in September and see how it works out." He said it in his "all done" voice, firmly. This was it!

My mother kept looking at me and said, "Helen doesn't agree but that's how it has to be." Her words were as final as Daddy's.

I left the room, hoping Riverside would burn down by September.

16

August and Never Summer were rapidly approaching.

First time I ever heard of that place was back in March, well before Chok-Do's arrival. It was while Daddy was talking about the camping trip we'd planned. When he said, "Never Summer," I swear I felt an unexplainable chill and in my mind's eye saw a place in the rocky peaks that was forever cold and barren.

We were at the table in the bright little breakfast room, with its chintz curtains and three Degas prints, just off the kitchen.

"It's in the Arapaho National Forest, bounded on the east side by the Never Summer Mountains. Seven thousand acres, mostly in the alpine, eleven or twelve thousand feet, though it drops to nine thousand in places. Not a tree anywhere in the alpine except for stunted growth. You ever see a tree a foot high that's a thousand years old?"

No, I hadn't. I didn't know foot-high trees a thousand years old existed. How weird. "Will we hike up there?" I asked.

"Sure."

He was excited even planning the trip, happy as a pup with three tails, all wagging at once. "If you look at this trail-system map, you'll see Never Summer above Lost Lake and Lake Ute."

I looked. Bordering the Continental Divide, next to the Rocky Mountain National Park, the wilderness had a crazy shape, with two camel humps. I saw some lakes. Icy, I'd bet; full of trout, I'd bet. My parents like to fish. It was a joint hobby.

I kept looking. Never Summer, in the alpine, always chilly and windy. Made me think of Switzerland and the Austrian alps that I'd seen in a "National Geographic" special.

Usually, we'd gone into national parks but the Park Service had passed a foolish regulation—no dogs allowed—and I was not about to go anywhere without Tuck and Daisy. Nor was I about to put them into a kennel. Never Summer was administered by the U.S. Forest Service and there was no such silly rule on that land.

"Looks rugged," my mother said, frowning a little.

"Is rugged," Daddy agreed, tapping a forefinger on a big color photo of the snow-topped peaks. Fluffy clouds slid along behind them.

"Will we camp up that high?" I asked.

He shook his head. "We'll stay in the subalpine for the first four days and hike up."

I knew the subalpine was below eleven thousand feet. The alpine, the treeless Arctic-like *tundra* land, was above eleven. Below the subalpine was the *montane,* the foothills.

"Then we'll drop down to about six thousand for the other three days."

We already had reservations at both campsites. July and August were always busy months in the national parks.

Long before "environmentalist" became the thing to be, my father cared for the land. He taught us to treat the earth gently and carry out every scrap of trash when breaking camp. "Let the wilderness be unchanged, as if we'd never passed through."

Luke, pausing by the table in his baseball uniform, said, "Have fun. Don't let the mosquitoes bite."

"Not many up at eleven thousand," Daddy said. "Maybe two that got lost, with big lungs."

Luke always had nosebleed problems above five thousand feet if we were going to stay more than a weekend, so he was going to the Y camp over on Catalina Island, as in the past, while we went on to Colorado. Stan hadn't made his plans as yet.

Massaging Tuck's yellow head, I looked at the volcanic peaks. They were streaked pink, yellow and gold below the snowcaps.

I said, "They're beautiful, aren't they?"

Mother said, hesitantly, "Umhuh. Somehow, they're also threatening. You could get hurt up there."

My father laughed. "Only if you slid down them on your behind."

On purpose? That wasn't likely, I thought.

I remember taking the dogs over to tell Mr. Ishihara we'd finally decided where to camp in August.

"Where to this time?" he asked.

"Never Summer Wilderness, in the Arapaho National Forest, in Colorado."

"So far away?"

"Well, we've done Yosemite, Sequoia and Kings Canyon . . ."

"But why in the world all the way to Colorado?" Mr. Ishihara shook his head in disbelief.

"Daddy likes to go to remote offbeat places. He wouldn't think of camping in the San Bernardinos or the Santa Barbaras," I said. " 'Nothing close around here. Besides, Never Summer is one of the few subalpine and alpine wildernesses left. It's almost like it was five hundred years ago,' he said."

"Drive all that way for just a week?"

"Two and a half days to get there. We'll see some of Arizona and some of New Mexico. He also likes long drives."

"You taking the dogs?"

"Absolutely," I said.

Mr. Ishihara shook his head again. "You know, I never was much for camping."

He spent most of his time off from Ledbetter's at the racetrack, either Santa Anita or Hollywood Park or Del

Mar. He had a system for betting on the horses; studied the jockeys and past races.

"I love to camp," I said.

He said, "If I had a family I might try it again. I haven't camped since the Boy Scouts." He was a fifty-year-old bachelor and had two gold teeth in his uppers.

I said, "How about your girlfriend? Does she like camping?"

He smiled widely. "Suzie likes the races."

A lady stepped up to buy fancy hydroponic white corn. You could buy midget carrots, shirataki mushrooms and sweet strawberries big as spinning tops from Mr. Ishihara.

I said, "I have to go."

Mr. Ishihara hugged me, as usual. "I'll try to win some money Sunday. Wish me good luck. The horses are still running at Santa Anita." I could see him going up to the betting windows in his porkpie hat.

He once had a mutt named Burney who chased sand fleas on the beach, doing figure eights. So he always bought Bernie's tip-sheet, the sheet that advised how to bet the races. Bernie picked a lot of winners, he said.

I said, "Good luck," and away we went.

Several days later I was back at Ledbetter's with the dogs and Mr. Ishihara said, "I checked into the Arapahos."

That was like him. He had a curious mind. All I'd have to do was mention something different or ask a question he couldn't answer and he'd read up on it. I'm surprised he wasn't president of Honda. He often went to the library branch near us to check out books. He was a lot like my father that way.

"They trace back to the Red River Valley in Minnesota and spoke Algonquian, as near as anybody can figure. Called themselves 'Inuna-ina.' They fought with the Utes."

"Spell that 'Inuna,' please," I said.

He looked in a little red pocket notebook and spelled it.

Daddy was always interested in things like that.

"They were related to the Blackfoot and Cheyenne tribes, but what's left of them now live with the Assiniboins in Montana, the Cheyennes in Oklahoma and the Shoshone in Wyoming at Wind River."

"You'll have to tell my Dad. Were they warriors?"

"Not really. They adopted the Ghost Dance religion."

"What's that?"

"The book didn't say. I'll have to do some more studying."

At nights at home, he read with his cat, Ichiban, curled in his lap, half-glasses perched on his nose, falling asleep sitting there.

17

Unexpectedly, Mrs. Gaines phoned to say she'd been in touch with a Korean family and they were interested in Chok-Do. They had a girl of eight and two older brothers. Could she bring the lady over?

Mother said, "Of course." Maybe this would be an alternative to the California School for the Deaf.

I was now willing to think that a Korean family, the exact *right* Korean family, might be better than the Riverside school, but I still hadn't given up my campaign to keep Chok-Do right here on West Cheltenham.

Mrs. Gaines and two Koreans arrived about eleven in the morning. The oldest one, Mrs. Shinn, looked like she was about my mother's age; the youngest one, very pretty, didn't look more than twenty. A college student, I bet. She was the interpreter. Mrs. Shinn spoke no English.

A tiny woman dressed in black, Mrs. Shinn had a hard wedge face and cold witch eyes, in my quick opinion. She wouldn't be a suitable mother for Chok-Do, I decided. On her left hand was what looked like a diamond as big as a piece of popcorn. Right away, I was against any transfer of him to her custody, same nationality or not.

He was out in the backyard playing with Tuck and Daisy and Mother told me to bring him in. Okay, I said, studying that hard wedge face and witch eyes. I went out.

There was no way to explain to him what might happen in the living room. How do you tell a deaf kid of six to make a big scene, stop his own possible adoption? To this date, he'd gone along with everything else—all the testing and the hearing aid—and he might just go along with Mrs. Shinn and live to regret it.

I decided to bring my friends, along with Chok-Do, racking my brains to figure out my own way to sabotage the meeting.

Mrs. Gaines said to Mrs. Shinn, "This is Chok-Do."

Who else did she expect it to be? Dracula? He was standing between the two dogs, facing the Korean ladies, puzzled look on his face.

I noticed that Mrs. Shinn didn't immediately cross over, kneel down beside him, hug him and talk to him in Korean, no matter that he couldn't understand. I'm sure he knew they were of the same race. Instead, Mrs. Shinn was examining him as if he were something to buy at auction. Then she seemed to be staring at Tuck and Daisy.

Ah-hah, maybe she was afraid of dogs? That's why she didn't go to him. Or maybe it wasn't her style to show affection in front of strangers. At any rate, I saw some hope.

I glanced at my mother. She was frowning slightly.

Suddenly, Mrs. Shinn began to jabber at the interpreter, who nodded and said to Mrs. Gaines and my mother, "Could we please ask you to take the dogs out of the room."

I was right. *Right! Right!* She was allergic or afraid of dogs or didn't like them, equally as bad.

Mother nodded, then looking my way, said, "Helen, take them outside."

I said, loud enough to be plainly heard, "People who don't like dogs *don't like people*." Then I took Tuck and Daisy by the collar and started out.

But I stopped by the dining room door, looked straight at Mrs. Shinn and said, "I hear that some people in Korea eat dogs. Is that right?" *I had heard it.* They sold and ate dog meat.

Mother said, sharply, "Helen!" Her eyes blazed at me.

"Is that right?" I repeated, as the interpreter translated to Mrs. Shinn.

"Helen!" my mother repeated. "Enough!"

I then proceeded through the dining room, into the kitchen and out the back door, in as dark a rage as I'd had in a long time. All the dog eaters in Asia should themselves be boiled in kettles.

I sat down on the garden bench near the bed of new poppies and fumed for a while, rubbing my fine animals for therapy.

About a half hour later, I heard voices at the front door and knew the visitors were leaving. I waited a few minutes and then went back into the house, asking my mother, "How did it go?"

"Not so well," she said, "thanks to you."

I had an inner grin but didn't display it. I looked over at Chok and held my fingers in a V. He grinned and held his up in a V.

"Did she ever come over and hug him?" I asked.

Mother said, sighing, "No."

I said, "I think I'll go over to Steffie's."

She said, "Take Chok-Do and the dogs with you. I have a headache."

And, for the time being, *that was that* for another family adopting my brother.

Later, Mother confessed, "I didn't like Mrs. Shinn, either." Then she laughed about it.

18

As a breed, Labradors, whether they be yellow, black or brown, are fine hunters, definitely not fighters, but most of the males can certainly rise to the occasion when called upon. I always knew that Tuck would willingly give his life to protect mine but on the gloomy Saturday in late July it wasn't my life at stake.

As we were going along Denham the light turned red at the intersection of Rosemont and a pickup truck came to a stop at the crosswalk. Out of the back plunged a squat brown dog, running silently, dragging a piece of rope, headed straight for Tuck and Daisy, teeth bared.

Immediately recognizing it as a pit bull, sometimes a killer dog, I yelled, "No! No!" and reached down to move them behind me. Lady Daisy was leading Tuck, of course.

Tuck sensed the trouble though he couldn't see it.

But he could hear it, I'm sure; smell it. And the fur rose behind his neck as he stiffened and growled.

I'd heard that you should be very careful in trying to break up canine fights. In the wild, twisting excitement even your own dog can bite you severely. And I had no stick to use on the angry pit bull. Lucky I didn't have one, he might have gone after me.

On it came—the owner obviously didn't know it had broken loose from the bed of the truck—launching at Daisy, sinking its teeth into her throat, slamming past my legs, knocking Tuck down. I went to my knees, still holding Daisy's leash as the pit bull ripped at her neck.

Then there was a roar and big Tuck suddenly had the pit bull by the nape of the neck and was shaking it, blood spraying from Daisy's throat. How he knew where to grab that chesty dog is a mystery but his teeth were sunk in, I saw, lifting the attacker off the ground. The pit bull let go of Daisy.

Frozen with fear, I was helpless as the attacker tried to twist his head around to get at Tuck.

Still on my knees, I let go the leash.

I guess my screams were loud enough to penetrate the cab of the truck, because the man jumped out and ran back to where we were.

He grabbed the dog by the ears, jerking it out of Tuck's mouth, then grasped the choke collar, towing it away, pit bull struggling to come back at us, still snarling.

Over his shoulder, the man said, "I'm sorry. She broke a rope." *She!* A female! A female did this!

As he stood there, Tuck's gray eyes were locked in the

direction of the sneak attack, fur still an inch high on his back. He was ready to do battle again, if necessary: to the death.

My legs felt like jelly as I got up.

Daisy slowly went down on her paws, shock setting in, I guess; then she rolled over, panting, her mouth open. She was bleeding heavily from the throat, which had been torn open. The sidewalk was turning bright red.

For a moment, I thought I might pass out from the sight of all that blood but somehow overcame the queasiness, knowing I had to get her to Dr. Tobin's hospital.

Several people had stopped and I asked a man to stay with them while I went home. The man said, "I'll try to stop the bleeding."

Fighting back tears as I ran, I was praying, "Don't let her die, God. Please don't let her die . . ."

Fortunately, my father was working in the garage that morning, fixing the power mower and minding Chok-Do, who was riding his trike.

Daisy was hurt bad, throat ripped, was what I blurted, tears flowing. I told him Daisy was down on the sidewalk three blocks away.

He quickly went into the house to get the car key, a towel and some just laundered dishcloths. In emergencies, Daddy most always stayed calm and reassuring. I put Chok in the front seat. His eyes were wide.

Denham and Rosemont was only a minute away and in another minute Daddy had lifted Daisy into the back of the station wagon, telling me to hold the dishcloth to her throat, talk to her, soothe her. My heart was pounding.

Chok's little face was pale.

We reached Dr. Tobin's hospital in another five minutes and transferred Daisy to an operating table. The vet made a quick examination, saying, "Whatever dog did this made a thorough job of it. It's very bad, Helen."

"Pit bull," I said.

"Figures," he said. "I'll have to put her to sleep to try and repair this, no promises. She's lost a lot of blood."

"There was a lot on the sidewalk," my father said.

It didn't take Dr. Tobin long to inject Daisy and put her under. As he was doing that, he said, "We need a transfusion."

"She can have my blood," I volunteered.

Dr. Tobin's laugh was brief. "Sorry, you don't qualify. She needs canine blood, A-negative."

"Tuck," I said, instantly.

"Maybe," said Dr. Tobin. "Bring him in. We'll take a sample."

Then he turned to my father. "You mind going to the lab?" He was readying to shave the ripped area with an electric razor. The fur was damp and matted dark crimson.

Daisy was motionless on the table, her breathing strained. I looked away from the ugly wound. The throat was laid open.

"Not at all," said my father.

So I went out to the wagon and brought Tuck in, telling him he could help save Daisy's life. She was so still and silent.

I turned my head as the vet drew out a test tube of

Tuck's blood, corking it. He gave it to my father, along with an address on Melrose.

Not wanting to see Dr. Tobin repair Daisy, stitch that deep slash, I went along to the lab with Chok and my father, thinking that it was Tuck who was in serious medical trouble only last year, having been hit by that car.

But I trusted Dr. Tobin to pull her through. On his wall were diplomas from the American Board of Veterinary Practitioners and the American College of Veterinary Surgeons. Yet . . .

"What's going to happen if the blood type isn't right?" I asked. I was so frightened. We were driving back to the clinic from the lab.

"I'm guessing that Dr. Tobin has a list of donor dogs."

"I hope," I said.

"Just trust him," my father said.

I tried to do that, saying over and over in my mind, Daisy will be fine! Daisy will be fine!

A few minutes after we arrived at Dr. Tobin's, his assistant came out into the waiting room to say that the lab had called. Tuck was A-negative and could safely give blood.

Thank God!

"I'll go get him," I said, moving out the door in a hurry.

Chok seemed bewildered at all that was happening, sitting on a chair with his feet dangling, looking from face to face. But he did know that Daisy was very sick.

Dropping the tailgate, I said, "Tuck, you've got it. I knew you'd have it."

He jumped down and I led him into the room where Daisy was still asleep on the operating table. She was patched up, still out. I could see the black nubs of stitches in her shaved throat.

The assistant wheeled another table in, a higher one, and Dr. Tobin placed Tuck on it, saying, "Okay, old boy, this isn't going to hurt one bit. We'll sedate you and take some fluid."

I admit to being squeamish about a lot of things— rats, snails that Luke put down my dress, snakes and so forth—and turned my head as Dr. Tobin inserted the needle into Tuck's right shoulder. My mouth was bone-dry.

"It'll take a few minutes until he gets drowsy," he said, then went on talking calmly: "Daisy lost an awful lot of blood. The pit bull cut a major artery."

I didn't like the sound of his voice.

"She'll be as good as ever?" I asked.

He didn't answer me directly. "I doubt she'll ever like pit bulls."

"They should be kept locked up," said my father.

"I agree completely," said Dr. Tobin, checking Tuck.

Then he said, "Okay, let's take some fluid. Blood types aren't all that critical in animals but I still like to use A-negative. You can transfuse to either A-positive or A-negative and not clash with antibodies under most circumstances."

I didn't even want to understand.

Soon, Tuck's good red corpuscles were flowing into a

plastic bag on a stand as I stroked his head, talking to him. He didn't make a move. In fact, by the time the blood was transferred his eyes were closed.

Chok-Do had come into the operating room with us and he wasn't nearly as squeamish as I was. While I petted Tuck his little hand was soothing Daisy, who was still unconscious from the injection. He was making one of those strange sounds.

A few minutes later, the blood bag was attached to an IV pole and Tuck's A-negative was flowing into Lady Daisy.

Dr. Tobin was constantly monitoring her but not saying very much. There was a grave look on his face.

"How is she doing?" I asked.

His eyes met mine. "Not very well, Helen. She's in a deep shock. She lost too much blood."

About ten-thirty her breathing stopped and my world came apart.

We had Daisy cremated at a place on lower Melrose, and the following Sunday, all of us went to Point Dume State Beach, north of Malibu, to scatter the ashes. Mr. Ishihara went with us.

I think my parents had in mind that it might be a healing place for me but it wasn't. It was a place of memory. We'd brought the dogs there the past winter and they'd happily romped. It was a place where Tuck could go full-speed without bumping into things. He'd only done that once, hitting a picnic bench. He'd gotten up, staggered a moment and then off he went with a big grin on his face.

This day he seemed lost without Daisy. All week, he'd seemed lost, those sightless eyes looking around for her. Both Chok-Do and I tried to be with him most of the time. It was evident to me that he was grieving for her.

The winter beach in California is sometimes grim, the water cold, the surf high and angry. White waves six or eight feet high roll in, pounding the sand, making it tremble. But I always liked the winter beach because few people were around, and often, in January and February, we'd see the last of the gray whales pushing south to the breeding grounds in Baja California.

This day the sea was sparkling and the surf was moderate; the sky was blue, for which I was thankful. This day I wasn't up to the grim winter beach.

The canine funeral home had given me a small wooden box, labeled Lady Daisy, and inside was a plastic bag with what remained of her. I walked away from the others and opened the box, tears flowing finally.

Mr. Ishihara walked over and said, "Which way would you like to go?"

I nodded south, calling for Tuck. He came up by my knees, locating me from the sound of my voice. Then I suddenly realized that Chok was there too. My parents and my brothers joined us, moving along the edge of the surf.

My father opened the bag for me and I took a handful of the ashes, tossing them into the water, seeing the glittering ocean and the sun through a film.

As we slowly walked along, each of us who loved her shared in the little ceremony, which I think Lady Daisy would have liked. At one point, I looked into the white-blue curl of a wave and thought I saw her out there, bounding along.

Ashes sent into the sea, we turned back north, sadness still there, but also a feeling of hope. I'd already contacted Mrs. Chaffey at the guide dog school, asking for another retired animal to take over where Daisy left off. Mrs. Chaffey promised she'd do her best.

Mr. Ishihara was beside me as we went back toward the station wagon. He said, "We're all on a journey, Helen, some for a long journey, others for a shorter one. Think of babies that die within a few weeks. Daisy's journey wasn't as long as it should have been. But think about all she did ... guiding for humans, then for Tuck ..."

I'd heard somewhat the same thing before about death, the journey thing, but from Mr. Ishihara it was different.

But the fact remained that Tuck was lost in darkness again, temporarily at least.

I noticed that Chok became even closer to Tuck almost immediately, hugging him more often, talking to him in "ryes" and "eeks" more often. It was Chok and Tuck, two handicapped "people," against the world.

19

As the days passed, now and then I'd look at all the Never Summer research stacked on my father's desk in the den. He kept adding information.

I read to Chok-Do and Tuck, though neither one of them understood a blessed word: "Underneath the peaks of Never Summer is a two-billion-year-old seabed with boulders of pink and yellow and sparkling gold. Millions of small rocks, called 'fell-fields,' are scattered around as if some giant machine had smashed them into pieces. Constant freezing and thawing shatters large rocks; then water seeps in and expands when it freezes, making room for more water, breaking more rocks."

Chok-Do was looking up at me as if he understood everything. "Winter winds whip away the warming snows and expose the multi-colored rocks."

One pamphlet said the song of the wind whines

almost constantly across Never Summer, swirling snow in winter whiteouts and causing the teeth of hikers to chatter, even in August, when we'd be going. Wind reaches a hundred miles an hour or more.

The Never Summer tundra, with its sparse patches of soil, was like the ground coverings of parts of Alaska and Siberia.

I went on: "There are pink snowbanks on the tundra, caused by communities of algae. They look weird yet inviting. The rangers call it 'watermelon' snow and, in fact, it smells and tastes like the real thing. But like other things on Never Summer, watermelon snow is deceiving. It concentrates airborne radioactivity, not good for man or beast."

I gazed down at Chok. "In other words we don't eat the watermelon snow."

The plants up there were purple sky pilot and whip-root clover and avens, "yellow roses of the tundra," and buttercups, blossoming many inches under the snow, their vivid colors lasting but six to eight weeks.

Daddy said that many were "belly plants." To see them, you needed to be on your belly.

I read on: "Hardy to the weather, they are still so delicate that a scuff of boot can destroy ones that are fifty years old. Some plants are estimated to be a thousand years old, like the stunted trees."

I said to Chok, "Don't step on any," then continued reading: "The small animals are yellow-bellied marmots, cousins of woodchucks, and pikas and gophers. During the brief summer they are hunted by weasels and coyotes. The bigger animals are deer, elk, bighorn sheep, mountain lions and black bears. Up in the sky, which is sometimes dazzling blue, other times closed in by fluffy, drifting clouds, are golden eagles, falcons and ravens."

I said to both of them, "Stay away from the mountain lions and the bears."

The days ticked off the calendar, Never Summer coming closer with each tick.

20

"We head for Colorado tomorrow."

"Your father hasn't changed his mind? Go to the Grand Canyon, instead? Just sightsee?" Mr. Ishihara asked.

"Nope, he hasn't changed his mind. And we've been to the Grand Canyon before. Not to camp, though."

"Well, be careful up there in those wild Rockies."

"We will be. We always *are* careful. You know my father."

Mr. Ishihara nodded. "Tell him to drive carefully, just the same. All those tourists on the road this summer. There are some crazy drivers out there."

"He's a very careful driver," I said.

I stood there just thinking, finally asking, "You worried about us?"

He looked up gravely. "Yes. I don't know why, but I am." His dark eyes showed concern.

"We'll be back here in one piece," I promised.

He nodded again, smiling this time. "I'm sure. I'm as American as Dwight D. Eisenhower but I still have this sticky Japanese blood in me. We think we see into the future darkly. Who do you think started reading tea leaves? Not the gypsies. We did it ten thousand years ago."

"You once told me that you thought reading tea leaves was nonsense."

"That's correct, I do. But I still read them," he said, smile changing to a wide grin, one gold tooth shining.

Shaking my head, I said, "I sometimes have trouble following you."

"I have the same trouble," he said, grin widening. "Okay, you go to Colorado tomorrow. I go to the racetrack Sunday. There's a two-year-old filly named Tokyo Tulip running in the third at Del Mar. I'm putting sixty dollars across the board on her."

"Who's riding her?" He'd taught me some of the jockey names.

"Willie Shoemaker."

"Then you don't need tea leaves," I said. Willie Shoemaker won most of the time, I remembered.

He nodded, still grinning. Then his expression changed as he looked down at Chok-Do. "Anything new on him?"

"Nope. He's still headed for Riverside and that deaf school in September."

"Maybe it's for the best." Mr. Ishihara reached over and scrubbed the crisp black crew cut affectionately. "I was thinking about him the other night. All the things he can't hear that we take for granted. Telephone, alarm bells, sirens. He can't hear a fire crackling. He lives in a dangerous world."

I'd never thought about it that way. I heard myself saying, "Maybe Riverside is for the best." Yet, on second thought, I doubted that.

Saying good-bye, I headed home.

He called after me. "Take a picture of one of those thousand-year-old trees. I have to see that."

I said I would.

Next day, Luke was packed off to the Y camp about four-thirty, Mother driving him to meet the Y bus up on Metcalf Square. His last words to me were, "Don't get your feet twisted and fall off a mountain." In other words, you Clumsy klutz!

"I won't," I said, not bothering to kiss his cheek.

Stan was going to stay at the Carruthers', who lived on Denham, while we were away. This would be the first time Stan hadn't gone camping with us.

"I've got too much to do," he'd said. When I was seventeen and dating I'd probably say the same thing.

So that part of our trip, Luke and Stan, was all set.

Taking Tuck and Chok for a walk at five, earlier than usual, I went by Steffie's house to say my good-bye to her.

The Pyles were going back East to visit her grand-parents in Michigan the second week in August. She wasn't excited about it. Steff was an only child. There were advantages and disadvantages to that. I suffered with Luke and Stan but still wouldn't have traded them.

"In a way, I wish I was going with you," Steff said. "I don't know a soul in Ann Arbor."

Last time she went to Michigan she'd spent a lot of time by herself in the university pool.

"Maybe you'll meet a good-looking boy?"

That brightened her a little.

We talked on for another ten minutes, then hugged each other.

Daddy again had the Never Summer information spread over the breakfast-room table that night for a final check. Maps, trail guides, the picture books.

As usual, we'd tow our twelve-foot aluminum boat. Most of the camping gear—big nylon tent, cookstove, cots, sleeping bags, utensils, etc.—collected over the years, would go into the boat. Food also in there. The rest would go on the roof of the rented four-wheel drive station wagon.

My father and mother didn't bring the outboard on trips such as this one. Motors weren't allowed on many of the lakes, especially the smaller ones in the subalpine. There was always the danger of oil or gas leaking.

"And, frankly, the wilderness doesn't appreciate the noise, either," Daddy said. It was as if the woods and rocks and tundra had eyes and ears.

They'd usually row out in the early mornings and late evenings, the best fishing times for trout—the cutthroats and rainbows—limiting themselves to two fish each, throwing all others back, using barbless hooks so the caught fish wouldn't be badly injured.

Sometimes I'd go along, though I didn't care all that much about it. Fishing tended to bore me after a while. I thought maybe when I was older I'd take a liking to it. Maybe I'd have a boyfriend who liked to fish?

Looking at the checklist, something Daddy always prepared for each trip, three heads bent over it, we talked for a while, Chok settled before the TV.

Then taking all the various picture books and information to bed with me, I read for more than an hour.

Sit beside a rushing stream and close your eyes. Watch a lodgepole pine sway against an azure sky. Listen to the rustle of leaves caused by a chipmunk's scurrying. Breathe the cool, fresh air of an evergreen forest.

I was roasting. Los Angeles was suffering a heat wave that week and the temperature in my room had to be eighty degrees at 10 P.M. I couldn't wait.

The photos of the jagged spires and mountain meadows were always breathtaking and cooling. Rugged land, as Daddy had said, with switchback trails that zigzagged into dizzy heights.

The Forest Service said *PLEASE: Walk gently on the trails* . . . (that we'd do).

Blend into the environment and travel quietly . . . (no problem).

Prepare carefully for lightning storms, sudden blizzards, rock slides, bright sun and possible injuries. Let someone at home know your plans . . . (Stan and Luke knew exactly where we'd be).

Turning off the light, I thought about the Never Summer Wilderness for a long time, excitement building.

Suddenly, I was on a subalpine switchback trail with Chok-Do and Tuck, who was no longer blind. I didn't even consider that strange as we slowly climbed. My parents weren't along and neither was Lady Daisy. Nor was that strange. So long as Tuck could see, Daisy didn't need to be with us.

The sky was azure blue with clouds drifting along the peaks, just like the color photo. Sun brilliant; air cool. How beautiful and lonely up here, I thought.

We were going along a ridge and below us was a steep slope covered with flat rocks about six inches wide. They looked like brown saucers. Talkative Chok was jabbering away. He could now hear and talk. He reminded me of the chipmunks we'd seen earlier on the trail.

Chok was on my right side, Tuck behind us, when I heard him scream, shrill and frightened.

I turned.

He was going down the slope on his back, the saucer-like rocks sliding with him. Yelling, he was sliding, sliding.

Tuck went charging after him and he also slid along on the plates.

I started down the slope, feet going out from under me, carried along with the clinking brown saucers.

Just as I reached the edge of the slope, where it

dropped off into a deep canyon, I saw Chok and Tuck below me, bloody broken bodies on giant boulders. They were dead, I knew. Mr. Ishihara had been right.

Bathed in sweat, awakened by my own screaming, I was aware that my mother was in the room, turning on the light. Then Daddy came in.

Mother asked, "Helen, what's wrong? What's wrong?"

It took a moment to realize that the rock-covered slope wasn't real; Tuck wasn't dead. Neither was Chok.

"Nightmare," I said, weakly. Mr. Ishihara's forecast.

Mother sat down on the edge of the bed, reaching for my hand. "It must have been a bad one."

"Very bad," I said.

It was the most awful nightmare I'd ever had but I didn't tell them about it just then. I wanted to sort it out. My heart was still slamming.

"You're okay now?" she asked.

I nodded. "I'm all right," I said.

I got out of bed, changed my soaked nightgown and went to the john, looking in on Chok, who was deep asleep.

Tuck was in there, sleeping peacefully, safely.

I did too after a while. Not entirely peacefully but safely in that room on Cheltenham, far removed from Never Summer.

At early breakfast, Mother looked at my father for the longest time and then said, "I must have stayed awake for two hours. Maybe we should call off the trip? Go some other place."

"What? Because of Helen's dream?"

"Premonition, Tony. Premonition!"

"Come on, Barbara. That's not like you. At this last minute?"

"Maybe it's too dangerous up there?" She glanced over at Chok.

"Oh, come on," he said. "She was reading all that wilderness stuff before she went to sleep." He looked over at me. "Isn't that right?"

I said it was.

Then he looked back at my mother. "You could have had the same dream, Barbara."

I said, "Mother, that's all it was. Just a dream. I dream all the time." I didn't want to be the cause of them canceling the trip.

"Okay," she said, but not convincingly.

No roads cut through Never Summer Alpine, the Forest Service booklet said. Just the two main hiking trails and some dead-end scenic-view offshoots. There were no fences, no signs, so you never knew when you'd stepped over the invisible boundary and on to the *fellfields,* that area of tiny ice-split rocks.

"You hike past the big-tree timberline, then come into the Elfin Forest, or *krummholz,* a German word, where the ancient scant woods are in miniature, knee-high gnarled and twisted fir and spruce, pruned by wind-driven sand and ice, all the surviving branches on the leeward side. You have arrived in a strange place!"

21

We crossed a lot of Colorado on U.S. 70 and then turned north in late afternoon on 40 to go to Granby, last-minute shopping place before heading into Never Summer on Baskins Gulch Trail, an old mining and lumbering road named after a prospector-settler.

"You sure you have enough dog food?" Daddy asked, craning his neck around. He was wearing a Dodger's baseball cap, not looking very much like a prominent electrical engineer.

"Maybe not," I said.

On the long ride from Montclair, not having the faintest idea where he was going, Chok had amused himself with coloring books when he wasn't looking out of the window. At times, I'd turn his head so he could see my lips, and tap the drawings, saying slowly, "Horse, horse, horse . . ." or "Rabbit, rabbit, rabbit . . ."

hoping he'd try to say the word. A sound did come out but it certainly wasn't horse or rabbit.

My mother had rotated around in the front seat each time to watch us and listen.

I'd been thinking about September, a few days less than four weeks away, and Chok-Do going to that deaf school in Riverside. It seemed inevitable now and so unfair to him. I'd thought about us driving away, leaving him there in the brick dormitory with two other little boys, him watching us go but unable to understand why.

I'd thought about the look that would be on his face, one that we might never forget. But I had more or less sadly accepted it by now, Chok-Do's fate, and seldom talked about it anymore.

Once, crossing Arizona, I brought it up, saying what a shame it was that we couldn't accept Chok *and* his deafness.

There was silence in the car.

I said, "Tuck will really miss him."

Mother said, looking back at me, "Let's don't ruin this vacation."

I dreaded the coming of September.

Tuck? He'd slept most of the way, doing it expertly, sprawled on a couple of old blankets behind the backseat. Every so often we'd made a bathroom and exercise stop for him. He was always a good traveler.

Chok often climbed into the back to be with him, scrubbing his neck, chattering to him.

Oh, how I missed Daisy not being back there.

Granby, on the tracks of the Denver Rio Grande and

Western Railway, isn't much of a town, most streets named after precious stones, but we spent the night there at the Blue Spruce Motel. Then, in the morning, topped off supplies at the supermart, including a few more cans of dog food, and went to the Sulphur District ranger station to check on road conditions once we left the hardtop.

"Never Summer, eh?" said the ranger. "Well, not too many people go up in there."

"That's exactly why we're going," said my father.

"Roads are okay up to Baskins Gulch Trail," the ranger said. "After that, no guarantee. I think you'd be better off going to Lost Lake Trailhead, come off 125, then pick up Cougar."

"Seems a long way around to get into Never Summer. Why can't we just come off 34, then pick up Baskins below Kawuncheehe . . . ?"

The ranger, a tall, skinny man with a big Adam's apple, shrugged. "Bumpy, either way, mister."

"I figured that," Daddy said. He thanked the ranger and said to us, "Let's roll."

We departed the Forest Service office a few minutes later and got on Route 34, going past crowded Lake Granby and Shadow Mountain Lake, leaving civilization at Grand Lake, rolling north, with the twisty-turny Colorado River, not much more than creek-size, off to the left.

Going by Grand Lake, Daddy waved his head toward it and said, "Indians say that it's haunted."

In the words of Luke Ogden, here we go again. I asked, "Why?"

"The Utes and Arapahos had a battle on its shore and to get away from the fighting all the women and children went out on rafts. A big wind came up and all of them were drowned."

"What a terrible story," my mother said.

"No Indian ever went out on that lake again, afraid of spirits."

Ghost Dance religion? I remembered Mr. Ishihara talking about the Arapahos.

"Any more stories like that?" I asked.

"None that I can think of," he said, laughing, turning on a Denver radio station, treating us to Andy Williams.

Past three widely scattered cabins, we crossed the little river and went west on Baskins Gulch Road, if it could be called a road at all. It was more a continuous pothole.

"Another fourteen miles," said my father. The day was lovely.

As the ranger had warned, we did "bump" along. The station wagon pitched and lurched and creaked, Tuck bouncing all around in his tight space. At not much more than five miles per hour, we crept past thick stands of spruce and fir and lumber pine, past loud-gurgling musical white-water creeks and their willow marshes. Even in late July, snow patches could be seen in the damp, dark forests. In other places the ground was covered with wild blueberries.

Also in the shade was Jacob's ladder, with sky-blue blossoms, and yellow arnica, moss and ferns. I'd learned about the flowers and trees, courtesy of my mother, from past camping trips.

In the sunny areas, we could see brilliant dark pink fireweed. There was vivid color everywhere and the chill air was so fresh and clean and moist that it almost hurt to breathe in after smoggy, hot Los Angeles. Down in the dry montane the older ponderosa pines had smelled like vanilla. Up here the trees gave off a pungent odor.

Now and then, at a distance, we'd see elk or mule deer feeding. They climbed to the subalpine meadows in the summer to get away from people and feast on the upper grasses.

I wondered if Chok-Do had ever seen land like this, cupped in glaciers. Korea had mountains, I knew.

There was a vantage point at a place called Paiute Vista and we stopped for a while.

I went around to the back of the station wagon, letting Tuck jump out. He went over to a fir to lift his leg.

Chok-Do slid out and looked around, as I did, awed by the scenery.

Looking to the east, my father nodded up to the rocky, snow-capped cones above us, saying, "Indian peaks—Pawnee, Ute, Arapaho, Comanche." They were jagged white spires. I almost expected to see a warrior of old, in battle headdress, on his pony.

"It's wilderness, all right," my mother said. We were all feeling small and insignificant.

I noticed that Chok-Do was entranced with the

peaks, his eyes locked on them. *Pawnee, Ute, Arapaho, Comanche.*

I turned him so that he could see my hands and signed, "Large, great, big, enormous, huge, immense."

My "L" hands—thumbs up, facing each other, fore-fingers half-extended, other fingers tucked down—now drawn apart, I nodded toward the spires, saying, "Big, big, big."

He smiled and looked back at the peaks, though I knew he didn't understand "big." He smiled, anyway, as if he realized I was trying to get some kind of message through. Oh, well.

Climbing back into the station wagon, we crept slowly upward.

Daddy said, "We're down in a valley at about nine thousand six hundred feet, according to the map. On the horizon, up there, is Mount Bowen, at over twelve thousand feet, and to the left is Ruby Mountain, also over twelve thousand feet."

They were both snow-capped. The Continental Divide skirted Ruby.

I'd read that the Never Summer Range also included half of Baker, Stratus, Nimbus, Cumulus, Howard and Richtofen. They marched up in awesome twelve-thousand foot humps all the way to Thunder Pass.

22

Lake Ute, a *tarn* shaped like a small harp, large end to the east, trees down to cold water's edge, finally came into view. The lake marked the beginning of Never Summer's camel-back shape. There was an Airstream trailer with Oklahoma plates, several campers and four tents around our end of the lake as we pulled into Space 8, by the Airstream, the few campers in residence waving to us.

Two hounds, tied up by the trailer, barked as we arrived, and a big, raw-boned woman opened the Airstream door to shush the dogs and yell, "Welcome," to us. She looked friendly.

Tuck soon met the hounds, both females, the usual sniffing investigations taking place. Peace would reign in the dog community. No males to compete with him.

I saw a small playground area with several swings, a slide and sandbox not far away and pointed it out to

Chok-Do as we began to unpack and set up camp. His face lit up and over he went.

Over to the left and beyond the trees, beyond the playground, was a "boulderfield," a weird-looking area that seemed to be about a mile long and a mile wide, treeless. Some of the boulders were taller than Chok. It looked like the gods had used it for a bowling alley.

"How did that get there?" I asked my father.

He shrugged. "I haven't the faintest. Leftover from a glacier action?"

The boulderfield was bordered on the south side by Cougar Creek, the map said. It was a lazy stream that came down from the mountaintops and fed Lake Ute.

Erecting the tent, setting up the camp stove, putting up the cots and arranging the food took the better part of an hour. Then we went for a walk around part of the lake, Chok tagging along in his bright red parka and red cap, Tuck on the leash.

Late afternoon sun began to light the peaks, turning them orange as we came back to Space 8. Soon my father slid the Sears boat off the trailer into the water, placing rods and reels and fishing tackle aboard, along with a dip net. For bait, they usually used orange or pink salmon eggs, little balls of shredded cheese. My mother was just as good at catching trout as he was.

"Wanna go, Helen?" she asked.

I shook my head.

"C'mon, tie Tuck up," my father urged. "We'll take Chok out."

I begged off. Instead, I went on a wood-hunting expedition while the fisher folk rowed out on Lake Ute.

Three times I returned to the camp with an armload for the evening fire. Next to early morning, with the smell of bacon frying, coffee boiling, evening was my favorite time in the wilderness.

That chore done, I walked over to the boulderfield to take a closer look. Little ones, big ones, of all shapes and sizes, they were scattered around in the square of land that sloped up into more trees. There wasn't a blade of grass or even a weed to be seen anywhere. It was spooky out there, looking like the back side of the moon. I said to Tuck, "Maybe this is where that Ghost Dance religion held meetings?"

I walked along the banks of rocky Cougar Creek for fifty or sixty yards, spotting some small trout in the pools, reminding myself to tell my father.

Returning to camp, I sat down in one of the beach chairs we'd lugged along and opened the guide for the trail system that led to the tundra. Flying Cloud sounded exciting for tomorrow.

About an hour later I could see the boat coming across the lake, could hear the thump of the oarlocks and voices in the dusk stillness. It was suddenly a comforting sound.

Soon, the boat closed on the shore and I went down to meet them, Tuck tagging along.

"Look what we have," Mother called out happily, holding up a string of four nice trout, breaking the deep quiet. Tuck barked at the sound of her voice, and I shushed him down.

"We caught a dozen," she added. "The lake is loaded."

Her voice seemed to boom all over the little valley and I was tempted to tell her to lower it, not disturb the peace, though she wasn't shouting.

The bow slid up on shore and they got out, Daddy saying, "You missed it! Oh, boy, they hit like hungry sharks! I picked the right place. Chok hooked up twice."

"I'll go out in the morning," I said.

My father tossed the anchor twenty or thirty feet up from the waterline, hooked it in the earth, so the boat wouldn't drift out, and we trooped up to the campsite, him saying, "Let's get a fire going, open the bar, peel some potatoes, make a salad . . . fresh trout from an ice-cold alpine lake for dinner, main course." He was loving it.

He went back into the woods several hundred feet to scale and gut the trout, carrying a shovel and a knife. The shovel was to bury the entrails, like good campers. I started the fire and my mother went about peeling the potatoes. Chok was going back and forth on the swings.

Soon, the campfire flickered in our faces, reddening them as we ate, mostly in silence. Subalpine cold had gripped the valley and Lake Ute. The night passed quickly.

23

Daylight edged down into the valley, Lake Ute "smoking," fog rising off it in gray fingers, and nearing six, we took the boat out and fished for almost an hour, cutthroats slashing at the bait as soon as it hit the water. I went along this time and enjoyed it, pulling in trout after trout, releasing all but the last one, a fine four-pounder.

Back ashore, we had a leisurely breakfast of pan-fried fish and skillet potatoes and mushrooms, then laced up our hiking boots and strapped on the rucksacks. My father checked the government green and brown topographical map and stuck the Never Summer trail guide into his hip pocket. Then we headed up Flying Cloud's zigzags for the alpine tundra about eight o'clock. The sky was clear and sunny, I remember, with some high, fluffy white clouds to the east.

Tuck walked along at my knees, having no idea where he was. Chok was by my side.

"This is really what it's all about," Daddy said, grinning widely, as we climbed in the fresh coolness. There was a sixteen hundred foot difference in the elevation between Lake Ute and the top of Flying Cloud.

We hiked up toward the pass, my father frequently carrying Chok-Do on his back, a chore he said he didn't mind. The day was again perfect—clear, warm and sunny, I remember.

Deer were everywhere along the aspen-filled slide areas and Chok-Do, bouncing along, laughed at them, pointing, saying something like, "Awk, awk." His wide grin said he was enjoying himself. He sounded like a parrot.

Yellow-bellied marmots and pikas, which look a lot like rabbits, were also thick on the slides as well as closer to the trail. The woodchucks sunned on the rocks and whistled at us as we went by.

"Get that out of your mind," I said to Tuck. He could hear the woodchucks and wanted, in the worst way, to get at them.

Twice, golden eagles soared overhead, their neck feathers glistening in the early sun.

Mother said, "Hey, look," as one plummeted down and then broke his fall by spreading wings just short of earth, seizing a small animal, rising back to the heights.

Daddy said, "They can see a rabbit from two miles away."

A little later, we spotted four or five bighorn sheep on

the steep rocky slopes of one peak and watched them for a few minutes.

"That must be some chase up there when a mountain lion goes after them. Imagine bounding over those rocks," he said, passing the binoculars.

We climbed onward and upward.

The air was thinning with each step and our breathing was starting to become labored. A "real lung-popper," the guide book said. The thin air also gave us a full dose of the sun's glare. We were wearing dark glasses, looking like skiers.

None of us were saying much. Mountain hiking doesn't lend itself to a lot of talking. It is for looking and thinking how good it is to be alive.

Finally, we came to the edge of the tundra, with its miles of wildflowers and the *krummholz*, the twisted, gnarled Elfin Forest, the miniature forests of spruce and fir, those thousand-year-old trees that were barely knee-high, hiding behind rocks to dodge the fierce winds.

"You ever seen anything like those tiny trees?" Daddy asked.

I hadn't. Mr. Ishihara would be impressed when I took the photos over to Ledbetter's.

I'd never been in such a strange land—the high peaks, the Lilliput trees and the vivid colors of the flower blankets. It was like a real Fantasyland.

At the top of the trail and the entry to the tundra was a Forest Service sign that said LIGHTNING HAZARD in bright yellow letters. Another sign, white letters on black, said what to do in case you were caught out in the open during lightning: "Run for the nearest forest but don't pick a lonely tree to stand under. If you can't make it, lie down in the deepest depression you can find, hopefully one without water in it. Stay away from piles of rocks and any piece of metal. If you're wearing a jacket take it off and place it beneath your body for insulation."

"Read it, Helen," my father ordered.

"I already did," I said, aiming my camera at the *krummholz.*

I tied Tuck at the base of the Lightning Hazard sign so he wouldn't gallop out over the sensitive tundra, ruin anything.

The wildflowers were dazzling in reds and yellows and pinks and blues and oranges, stretching up into the rocky ramparts beneath the snowcaps. We soon spread apart and stork-walked from rock to rock among them, trying not to step on any plant, my father guiding Chok.

A light wind was blowing, nodding the heads of the larger flowers.

At one point, Mother said, "I feel like it's sacred up here."

I remember turning back and looking at her. Yes, sacred.

She said, "I almost feel we shouldn't be intruding." She'd stopped walking and was sitting on a small boulder, a look of awe on her face.

It did feel like we were intruding on another planet.

The alpine chill, the bobbing heads of the wildflowers, the silence except for the marmot whistles and the croon of the wind made it seem like we were cut off from every other human on earth. I shivered, remembering the bad dream.

Having gone up almost four miles on the switchbacks, we started down again about eleven-thirty and reached the trailhead flats, the wide boulderfield to the south of the campsite, an hour later.

Lunch—leftover grilled trout from last night and French bread—was soon on the thick-boarded table. Then one by one, Chok-Do first, we bedded down for a post-noon nap. The morning's walk and altitude had left us yawning. I put Tuck into the station wagon, into his usual bed behind the backseat. Too many small enticing animals were in the woods nearby to let him roam free.

Then I slid into my sleeping bag. On the next cot was my temporary brother, already slumbering.

What happened next was as predictable as the coming of night: I awakened about forty minutes later and there was no small body on the cot next to me.

He's gone out to play with Tuck, I thought. Or to the swings.

I got up, put on my boots, grabbed my jacket and went outside.

Tuck was still in the station wagon, slumbering nicely.

No Chok-Do within sight.

The Oklahoma woman in the Airstream in Space 7 came out of her trailer with a pan in her hands.

"Have you seen the little boy?" I asked.

"He took Tess for a walk. He sure doesn't say much. He just came up and unhitched her. Didn't even ask me."

"He can't ask you. He's a deaf-mute."

"You know I thought something was wrong with him but I'm not nosy."

"Which way did they go?"

"Out toward the rocky flats. Ol' Tess'll bring him back. She's a homing dog."

I looked out over the rust-colored boulderfield and didn't see the red-jacketed boy or Tess among them.

Debating about waking my parents, I thought as long as he'd gone out on the flats, didn't go up the trail or down it, wasn't skirting around the lake, he was probably all right, just exploring the boulders. Almost any kid would do that. And he hadn't been gone that long.

But recent experience with our wandering orphan told me to start looking and waste no time. I routed Tuck out of his dog dreams, wondering why he hadn't barked when Chok came out of the tent and untied Tess. I doubt if we would have heard him, anyway, from inside the station wagon.

Not five minutes away from the campsite the sun was suddenly blotted out by black clouds that had come over the peaks with the speed of a fast freight train. They were rolling and curling angrily. In the distance I could hear thunder and the wind had turned icy cold. What had been a beautiful mid-afternoon was now dark and forbidding, all in seconds.

About two minutes later the hound named Tess trotted by us, homing all right, running through the boulders from the storm, trailing her leash. Chok wasn't with her. What immediately worried me was lightning.

We'd been caught in two high-mountain storms on past camping trips and nothing on earth is as terrifying. *Nothing.* The noise alone causes your heart to drum; the sight of the wavering white-blue ropes of electricity takes your breath away. A woman was killed by a bolt in a Yellowstone parking lot.

It was as dark as twilight, the far-off rumbling continuing, and I said to Tuck that we had to find Chok-Do. Right now!

I looked up toward the Never Summer Peaks. Streaks of the white-blue were lancing out of the blackness. Distant thunder rumbled again.

Tuck understood. His nose was bent toward the ground as we went south through the boulders at a trot. With no Daisy to lead him, I steered him around the big rocks with the leash, trying to remember what Daddy had said about electric storms.

"Upstrokes," with lightning climbing from the ground upward to the clouds, were the most dangerous, creating fifty thousand degrees of heat in any conductor—a tree, a pile of rocks or a human body. "Downstrokes," which originate in the clouds, quickly lose their strength. Both are dangerous.

Traveling along the ground in what he called "step

voltage," the current fans out from where the bolt hits. Above all, lightning does strike twice in the same place. Over and over again, same trees, same rocks.

When we were caught out in the open in Yellowstone, I remember him counting the five-second intervals between the thunderclaps and the lightning to estimate how close the storm was passing.

The rumbles of thunder were not so distant now and there was no sign of a lost little boy in a red cap and jacket up ahead.

We ran on toward Cougar Creek.

Suddenly, the whole boulderfield seemed to lift off the ground with a boom so loud that I momentarily joined Chok-Do in deafness. The plateau turned sizzling blue-white as a bolt hit not two hundred feet from us, knocking us down. It was as if a bomb had been dropped.

As the noise echoed across the flats, I heard Tuck howl for the first time in his life—a deep, scared moan. I looked over at him. The hair on his back was standing straight up from static electricity.

Then rain and hail began to pelt down and I crawled over to see if he was all right. Down on his belly, chin flattened against the earth, he was both stunned and frightened.

Thinking that the lightning could strike again, I looked around for a low place and saw a hollowed-out spot about twenty feet away. Towing Tuck, I crawled over to it. It was against my father's safety rule to huddle with Tuck—people are supposed to separate during strikes—but I thought he might panic and run off.

I told him to stay down and waited for the next upstroke or downstroke. Two or three long minutes went by and then another boom rocked the earth and blinded us for a few seconds. But in the white flash I seemed to see a red smear up ahead.

Rain and hail increased for a few minutes, pounding our backs, and then, as if a heavenly faucet had been turned off, the fast-moving storm retreated from Flying Cloud Trailhead, leaving dripping noises.

Tuck raised his head and stared off toward Cougar Creek, sniffing. I knew he was hearing something I couldn't hear. *Chok!*

I said, "I saw something red up there when that bolt hit."

Tuck had already risen to his feet and off we went toward the creek bank, weaving in and out of the big boulders.

Three hundred yards, two hundred, and then even I could hear the faint bird-like "awks" and "ryes."

Finally, I saw him standing on the opposite bank of the creek, which was now raging. He was drenched and crying but alive, a tiny pitiful figure in the half-light.

The rocky stream, which had seemed so lazy and innocent the previous afternoon, had turned into a torrent, fed by rainfall from the peaks. It had been five or six feet wide; now it was ten or fifteen, frothing and churning, setting up a din.

Chok's face was milky and his eyes were popping. He was petrified.

"Stay where you are," I yelled to him, hoping my parents had been awakened by the storm and were now out searching for us. Not daring to leave the creek bank to get help, having no idea what he'd do—maybe try to wade across, follow me—I could only try to keep him over there.

Holding Tuck's leash, I yelled again, "Stay where you are," pointing at Chok's feet, trying to make myself understood. Useless effort. "Stay where you are!"

The wail of "ryes" continued, helplessness and panic all over his face. He seemed ready to cross.

Suddenly, Tuck's head was raised as he sniffed the damp air and then he "looked" to the right of Chok-Do. He began to growl.

I saw movement against the dark, green treeline, a four-footed blur of tan to the right of Chok-Do, about thirty feet behind him, my breath catching as I realized what it was. *Mountain lion!* Big one. Probably coming down from the peaks, running before the storm, and as frightened of the bolts as we were.

Tuck's growling became heavier and more threatening. He could smell the big cat, maybe even hear it, but didn't know what it was. Enemy, for sure. I held his leash tighter, wrapping it around my wrist so that he wouldn't do anything foolish.

"And, please God, don't let Chok see it," I said, barely breathing.

To this day, I'll never know why Chok turned his head at that instant. Maybe movement out of the corner of his eye; perhaps he sensed danger by watching Tuck. Whatever the reason, he spotted the cougar and screamed.

Then it all seemed like it was happening in slow-motion—Chok starting across the creek, stepping off into the roaring water, feet going out from under him, red cap spinning off.

I saw the top of his head disappear and then plunged in after him, forgetting I was tied to Tuck. Swimming mattered little in that millrace, which was a light chocolate color. The current carried us along like we were woodchips, my feet and legs bumping against rocks.

Chok was eight or ten feet ahead, off toward the left-hand bank, yelling in that high-pitched "eeeeeeee," his sound of terror, and suddenly I could feel big Tuck, always the water dog, swimming strongly, pulling me that way.

Then I hit a rock, head-on, and everything went black.

I awakened a little while later, flat on my sore back, to find Chok-Do staring down at me, his button nose not six inches from mine. I realized we were safely out of the water and on the bank. No repeat of that awful dream I'd had on West Cheltenham.

Chok looked okay. He said something to me in gibberish. I didn't know whether to kiss him or brain him. That kid had enough charmed lives for a dozen Koreans.

My head was throbbing and every muscle felt bruised.

I heard a voice asking, "You all right, young lady?"

I looked toward the voice and saw the raw-boned woman from the Oklahoma Airstream standing there.

"I'm okay, I think. Where's Tuck?"

"Sitting right here."

I looked over at him. He was wetter than I was, yellow fur matted.

"He's okay too," the woman said. "Your Mom and Pop got everybody at the camp out searchin' for you. I come down here by the creek just in time to see you three ridin' the rapids, that dog holdin' the boy in his teeth an' towin' you. Must say I thought you were dead. That's a nasty bump on your forehead."

"Feels that way," I said, touching it.

"You got knocked out. Wonder you're alive."

I agreed.

"That is some dog you have, blind or not. Quick as his feet touched bottom he dragged the two of you up here on the bank."

I also agreed to that, glancing over at Tuck. He was "some" dog, to say the least. He was squatting there as if he'd enjoyed the ride. He deserved a medal.

Just as I sat up, I heard a shout and knew it was Daddy. He was running toward us, along with my mother.

There was quite a reunion out by that roaring creek, as well as a useless severe lecture to Chok-Do Choi.

I went back to Campsite 8 on wobbly legs.

The weather turned fine again and we broke camp the morning of the fourth day to go down to the montane for our next and last reserved site. Nothing else happened at Flying Cloud, thank goodness. Chok behaved himself and didn't go further than the swings. Cougar Creek had taught him a needed lesson.

At Paiute Vista, we stopped again to take a look at the Indian peaks in all their glory—Pawnee, Ute, Arapaho, Comanche. The sun was glistening on their white tips, the air again cool, fresh, clean and dry. There was a goodness up there that reminded us why we'd visited Never Summer.

My mother had been unusually quiet since the lightning storm and the near tragedy that followed it. But I noticed she'd looked at Chok-Do in a different way; perhaps me too. Death had come too close.

All four of us were standing near one another. Taking her eyes off the peaks, glancing down at Chok, she said, ever so slowly, "I've decided to ask for a two-year leave of absence and stay home with Chok. Teaching is what I'm all about, isn't that right? I'm going to be the best signer in the state of California."

My father grabbed her and kissed her. I did the same thing after he got through.

It was the right place, this Never Summer Wilderness, for her to make such a decision—an "L" hands one: big, huge, enormous, immense.

I lifted Chok-Do up and hugged him, though he didn't know what all this hugging and kissing was for. I flashed the car salesman's V-for-victory sign at him and he flashed it back, with a grin, though he still hadn't the slightest idea what it meant: old Metal-Mouth Goggle-Eyes had won again.

Finally, I hugged my special hero Tuck. Had it not been for him . . .

Mother said, "I'll hire a sign language instructor to teach me."

"I've already talked to one," I said. "She lives in Redondo Beach. Sally Larrimer."

"I might have known," Mother said, laughing, shaking her head. "Sally Larrimer?"

As we got back into the station wagon to descend about eight more miles it seemed to me that the sun was brighter, the birdsong louder, the whole world a nicer place to be.

Now, I could go about my main business of finding a replacement guide dog for triumphant Tuck.

DATE DUE

MAY 3			
MAR 4		MAY 4 2004	
MAR 1 6			
	NOV 6		
JAN 2 2 2001			
	NOV 5 2001		✓
	MAY 2 0 2002		
	FEB 2 4 2004		
DEC 20 2000			
GAYLORD	JAN 1 1 2007	PRINTED IN U.S.A.	